W9-CND-315

ONE IS ONE
AND ALL ALONE

ONE IS ONE
AND ALL ALONE

ANTHEA FRASER

ST. MARTIN'S PRESS ☙ NEW YORK

THOMAS DUNNE BOOKS.
An imprint of St. Martin's Press.

ISBN 0-312-19309-2

First published in Great Britain by Collins Crime,
an imprint of HarperCollins*Publishers*

First U.S. Edition: December 1998

10 9 8 7 6 5 4 3 2 1

GREEN GROW THE RUSHES-O

I'll sing you one-O!
(Chorus) Green grow the rushes-O!
   What is your one-O?
One is one and all alone and evermore shall be so.

I'll sing you two-O!
(Chorus) Green grow the rushes-O!
   What are your two-O?
Two, two, the lily-white Boys, clothed all in green-O,
(Chorus) One is one and all alone and evermore shall be so.

I'll sing you three-O!
(Chorus) Green grow the rushes-O!
   What are your three-O?
Three, three, the Rivals,
(Chorus) Two, two, the lily-white Boys, clothed all in green-O,
One is one and all alone and evermore shall be so.

Four for the Gospel makers.
Five for the Symbols at your door.
Six for the six proud Walkers.
Seven for the seven Stars in the sky.
Eight for the April Rainers.
Nine for the nine bright Shiners.
Ten for the ten Commandments.
Eleven for the Eleven that went up to Heaven.
Twelve for the twelve Apostles.

ONE IS ONE
AND ALL ALONE

1

It was the time DCI Webb always enjoyed: the day's work was behind him; outside, the March winds blustered with their usual vigour, hurling the occasional handful of sleet against the windows, while here, in his little domain, all was warmth and peace – and Hannah had come for supper. Furthermore, since her flat was on the floor below, he wouldn't even have to brave the elements to take her home.

'You're looking very pleased with yourself,' she commented. 'What were you thinking?'

He grinned shamefacedly. '"East, West, Home's Best", or something equally corny.'

'Well, so it is.' She stretched out her legs to the gas fire's blatantly fake logs. 'Especially on an evening like this. I've been trying to guess what you've got in the oven; it smells delicious.'

'Spiced pork.' He topped up her glass. 'I'm having quite a social day today; I met Malcolm Bennett for lunch and we went to that new grill place.'

'Any good?'

'Yes, well worth a visit. Decor's a bit jazzy but the food's excellent.'

He frowned, staring into the dancing lights of the fire, and Hannah watched him curiously, aware that something was bothering him.

'Is he the one who recently remarried?' she prompted.

'Not all that recently – must be getting on for two years. But yes, that's Malcolm.'

Another pause. To break it, she said, 'And has it worked out?'

Webb sighed. 'I've been asking myself that. To be honest, I can't think why he married her. Carol was such a pretty little thing, with a sparkle almost to the end. This one's as stiff as a waxwork – no warmth about her at all.'

'His family's grown up, I suppose?'

'Yes, a son and two daughters. Tim and Sally are married and Jane, the youngest, lives with her boyfriend.'

'How did they take their father's marriage?'

Webb shrugged. 'He met Una less than a year after Carol died and they married three months later. It's my bet the kids resented her from day one. But they were all living away from home and I suppose he was lonely, poor bloke.'

'You coped,' Hannah pointed out, 'without marrying the first woman who came along.'

'It's different after a divorce; I was glad to see the back of her!'

An oversimplification, as Hannah well knew, but she merely said, 'Has he hinted at problems?'

'Not specifically, but I've known him a long time. I was best man at his wedding. The first one, that is.'

'But not the second?'

'They don't have best men at register offices. It was wise not to marry in church, though; it would have brought back Carol's funeral, for all of us.'

'So what's she like, this new wife?'

'Tall, thin. Not pretty, certainly, though she has fine eyes and quite a striking face. But it's her manner that's off-putting – so stiff and formal.' He shook his head. 'Poor old Malcolm; I hope he's not bitten off more than he can chew.'

'Well,' Hannah remarked, leaning forward and putting her glass on the table, 'it might not be the most delicate observation in the circumstances, but he made his bed and now he must lie on it.'

'And I don't envy him that, either!' Webb commented, getting to his feet and going to check on the casserole.

Across the town Una Bennett, still at her desk, sat staring at the door, which was vibrating from its resounding slam. That was totally uncalled-for! she thought angrily. She'd been quite justified in her criticism and there was no need for Pat to fly off the handle like that, let alone give in her notice. Now she'd have to go through all the rigmarole of advertising and interviews, and it couldn't have come at a worse time, with that trilogy awaiting translation.

Well, there was nothing she could do this evening. She glanced at her watch: seven o'clock, later than she'd – She drew in her breath, eyes widening in consternation. Damn! The upset with Pat had made her forget it was Malcolm's birthday, and the family was coming to dinner.

Hastily she locked her desk, shrugged on her jacket and reached for the phone.

'Malcolm? Sorry, I've been delayed but I'm on my way now. Would you be a love and put the ducks in the oven? ... What? Yes, of course both of them. I should be home in half an hour.'

The lift seemed slower than usual, stopping on the first floor to let more people crowd inside. Reaching the ground floor at last, Una hurried along the passage to the door opening on the car park. It was raining – hard, icy drops that stung her face.

Head down, she hurried over to the car. Before her marriage, her flat had been only five minutes away; now, she had to negotiate the centre of town, always snarled up with traffic at this time of night, then face the twenty-minute drive to Lethbridge. Not to mention, when she finally reached home, the disapproving faces of the family.

She edged her way out on to King Street, switching her mind from office problems to the evening ahead. Barbara was coming, too, she remembered, filtering round Gloucester Circus: Carol's unmarried sister who, Una was convinced, had hoped, after a decent interval, to marry Malcolm herself. God, what a hornet's nest she'd married into! She'd been better off –

Her thoughts skidded to a halt and were firmly battened down. No, she hadn't meant that – not really. She was still fond of her husband, even if his set ways occasionally drove her to distraction.

Her eyes on the wet road, she thought back to their

meeting, on the coach trip to Scotland. Since all the other passengers were paired off, they'd been more or less thrown together, but after a day or so she'd found herself watching out for him. He was a big man – tall and broad-shouldered, his hair, still plentiful, fading barely noticeably from fair to grey. For the rest, a face that was pleasant rather than good-looking, and bushy eyebrows which were somewhat at odds with the twinkle in the eyes beneath them.

Almost inevitably they'd sat beside each other on the coach and again at dinner each evening at the different hotels en route. Since the tour had been organized by Prime Travel of Shillingham, it was no surprise to find he lived locally, in the neighbouring town of Lethbridge. What *had* surprised her was his job – a detective chief inspector.

That he was lonely was obvious, and he'd lost no time in telling her of the death of his wife and about his children and grandchildren. For her part she'd volunteered nothing, but his gentle yet persistent questioning had soon elicited the admission that she also lived alone.

It was his undivided attention that charmed her. She was not used to the company of men, possessed, as she well knew, no feminine wiles to snare them. But this kindly policeman seemed, to her astonishment, to find her attractive, and she was more than grateful.

Wondering anew what he'd seen in her, she glanced briefly in the rear-view mirror. Black hair in a short bob, dark eyes with strong, black brows: no obvious charms there. Nor, she noted wryly, had her brief marriage dispelled what she thought of as her 'spinster look' – an almost imperceptible pursing to her mouth, an air of resigned apartness.

It came, she thought now, from thirty years of being alone, for since her mother's death that was how she'd felt, whether or not there'd been others around. Her very name compounded it. When she was a child, her father had explained that Una meant 'one and only'; her parents had married late, and there would be no more children. In fact, 'One-and-Only' became his pet name for her – 'Come along, One-and-Only, time for bed!' Sometimes he'd call her 'Una-ique', which she'd gathered meant the same thing.

But her kind, joking father had died when she was thirteen, and her mother followed him five years later. Then it had been brought home to Una that she was indeed 'One and Only', with no one left who belonged to her. Without her work and her music, life would have been insupportable.

As she turned at last into her drive, still caught up in memories, she recalled an exchange which had taken place in an office where she'd once worked. To her comment, 'One can't do everything oneself!', that woman – what was her name? – had snapped irritably, ' "One"? Who or what is "One"?'

And Una had replied unthinkingly, ' "One is one and all alone, and evermore shall be so." '

She remembered being appalled at the accuracy of the quotation, and the woman, after a startled look at her white face, had gone out of the room.

Blocking off further reminiscences, Una turned off the ignition, gathered up handbag and briefcase, and went into the house.

The smell of duck wafted in waves of succulence from the open kitchen door. At least dinner shouldn't be too much delayed by her tardiness.

She pushed open the sitting-room door, and the conversation in progress stopped abruptly.

'Hello, everyone,' she said with forced brightness, conscious of their alert, watching faces. 'Sorry I was tied up, but I'm sure you've managed to entertain yourselves.'

Malcolm moved towards her and she pressed her cold face briefly against his warm one. 'Thanks for seeing to the ducks.'

'Is there anything else I can do?'

'You could lay the table, if you don't mind. Everything else is under control. I'll just run up and change.'

Before going upstairs, Una checked the oven, switched on the extractor fan, took the cheese out of the fridge, and closed the kitchen door behind her.

God, she could have done without this, tonight of all nights, she thought with exasperation as she hastily washed – no time for a shower. After a difficult day at the office, it would have been pleasant to have curled up with supper on a tray and an anodyne television programme. Instead, she had to produce a three-course meal for people who resented her very existence, and, what was more, smile while she did so.

Would they, she wondered, not for the first time, have objected to anyone their father had married? Was it because the wedding was too soon after Carol's death? Or was she herself the problem? She was well aware of her uncanny knack of antagonizing people, which she seemed unable to circumvent. Whatever the reason for their dislike, there was no way now to rectify it.

Swiftly she applied make-up, brushed her hair, slipped into a green silk dress, and, with a last check in the mirror, hurried back downstairs.

The meal, carefully chosen to include Malcolm's favourite dishes, was progressing smoothly. Una had given some thought to seating, and, while checking her husband's table-laying, had put neat little name-cards in each place. Barbara, she'd positioned as far from herself as possible, on Malcolm's right, which should please her, she'd thought caustically.

The plan seemed to be working well; as Jane's boyfriend, Steve, had been unable to come – no loss, in Una's view – the two sisters were seated side by side. There was not, she thought, watching them, a strong family resemblance; Sally, the elder, was a no-nonsense young woman with a firm chin, whose blonde hair was caught back in a tortoiseshell slide. Jane, at nineteen the youngest of Malcolm's children, was more vivacious, with a bubbly personality she inherited from her mother. She also had the Bennett fair hair, but hers was frizzled all over in the prevailing fashion which, to Una's eyes, looked as though it hadn't been combed in weeks. The two of them were engaged in animated conversation which produced an occasional burst of laughter.

Across from them, on Una's left, Sally's husband Neil sat silently between Barbara and Jenny, Tim's wife. Glancing at his closed, sullen face, Una felt the invariable twist of dislike. He was a pompous, arrogant young man, too handsome for his own good, who lost no opportunity to cause trouble.

Beyond him, Barbara was in the middle of a long story to

which Malcolm was listening, his head slightly bent towards her, and Una, continuing her analysis, turned her attention to them.

Barbara Wood was an elegant woman, who wore her chin-length grey hair in a straight bob. As Una watched, she laughed and hooked it back behind her ear with an almost girlish gesture. She had large, deep-set grey eyes, high cheek-bones and good bone structure, and though not as pretty as her sister's photographs, was well-groomed and attractive. Una wondered how long she'd been in love with Malcolm; possibly ever since Carol married him, which could account for her remaining single. Or possibly this was only because, like Una herself, Barbara was a career woman, teaching history at a private school in Shillingham.

And Malcolm? Una's eyes lingered reflectively on her husband. The last two years had not been without contretemps as two strong characters adjusted to living together. More volatile than he, there'd been times when his reasonableness infuriated her. At others, he'd reacted with an angry outburst at what he saw as her insensitivity. Perhaps all marriages were like that; she'd no way of knowing. But it did seem that those who embarked on it later in life had as a consequence more rocks to negotiate; the young tended to blunder on regardless, confident that love would see them through.

And hard on that thought came the realization that she didn't love Malcolm – probably never had. The suddenness of the revelation shocked her, and she was still adjusting to it when she became aware of her stepson's assessing gaze.

'A penny for them,' he invited unsmilingly. How much had he read into her study of his father? That last, disconcerting admission?

'Save your money, Tim!' she answered lightly. 'How's business going? Plenty of crowns and other lucrative treatments?'

Tim was junior partner in a dental practice. 'We're managing,' he said stolidly. 'What about you? You must be busy, if you even have to work late on Dad's birthday.'

Una hid her annoyance at the implied rebuke. 'We are busy,

yes, but it was a domestic matter that delayed me. Domestic to the office, that is.'

'Someone get the chop?'

Una flushed. 'Not exactly.' Unwilling to discuss her problems on this social occasion, she turned from him to his wife.

'How are the children, Jenny? We don't seem to have seen them for a while.'

'Fine, except that Lisa's playing up a bit. She decided she didn't want to go to nursery school and threw a tantrum when I insisted. She was fine once she was there – I phoned later to check – but we've had the same performance every morning. And of course each time Lisa cries, Sara-Jane joins in. It's like a parrot house.'

Una smiled. Jenny was her favourite member of the family, the only one who treated her normally.

At the far end of the table, Malcolm put down his spoon and leaned back.

'A lovely meal, dear. Thank you. In fact, I've done very well today; I had lunch with Dave Webb – did I tell you? We went to the Grill House in Carlton Road. Have any of you tried it yet?'

They shook their heads. 'How is Mr Webb?' Jane asked. 'Mummy always liked him, didn't she? She was sure he had a girlfriend, but could never find out who it was!'

'Your mother was an incurable romantic,' Malcolm said with a smile. There was a slight, uncomfortable pause, then he added, 'Dave's fine – and if he *has* a girlfriend, he certainly keeps her well hidden.'

'What was his wife like?' Sally asked curiously.

'Susan? Lord, I've almost forgotten. OK, I think, though she could be sulky if she didn't get her own way. We saw quite a bit of them in the early days.'

'He came to school last year,' Barbara commented, 'during all that cult nonsense. He handled it very well, I thought. I was quite impressed.'

'And it takes a lot to impress Auntie Barbara!' Jane declared impishly.

Everyone laughed, but Una was remembering the tall, lean man at her wedding. His appraising eyes had made her uncomfortable, and she recalled being glad their meeting was a social one. It would, she'd felt, be difficult to keep anything from him.

'So you went swanning off to lunch, did you?' Neil said unpleasantly. 'All right for some!'

'Oh, it wasn't purely social. We've had a sudden increase in shop raids, here and in Shillingham. Same MO each time, so we're doing a spot of liaising.'

'Over lunch at top restaurants; that would please the tax-payers!'

Malcolm held up his hands with a laugh. 'I'm sorry I mentioned it! The Grill's hardly a "top restaurant", but if you must know, I invited Dave to lunch to celebrate my birthday, and the Brown Bear, which is our usual haunt, didn't quite fit the bill. No pun intended!'

The family groaned. 'You're getting worse, Dad!'

Una could feel her smile becoming fixed. This casual family banter was a closed book to her and she was out of her depth. To put an end to it, she pushed back her chair.

'If everyone's finished, shall we go through for coffee?'

In the sitting-room the groups re-formed and she found herself unavoidably next to Barbara. Being of an age, they should have been friends, but Una was aware it wasn't only the fact that she'd married Malcolm which prevented this. Something in her manner had alienated Barbara at their first meeting, and their relationship remained formal. Now, however, sipping her coffee, Barbara turned to her.

'I see the Choral Society's giving a concert in Steeple Bayliss. Are you taking part?'

Gratified by the unexpected interest, Una nodded. 'Yes; it's quite a big work, so the two societies have combined. We've been rehearsing for months.'

'Which means,' grumbled Malcolm good-humouredly, 'if she's not working late at the office, she's out singing. This was the first decent meal I've had in weeks!'

'Will you be going to the concert?' Barbara asked him.

'Lord, no! Music's not my line, as you know.'

'He prefers football, which isn't *my* line,' Una said. 'Still, we wouldn't want to live in each other's pockets.'

Barbara carefully did *not* raise an eyebrow; it must have taken an effort. 'All the same,' she countered, 'it's nice to have shared interests.'

'We both enjoy walking,' Malcolm put in quickly, 'don't we, dear? At weekends, if I'm not on duty, we often make a day of it – set off cross-country and have a pub lunch somewhere.'

Una smiled agreement, but his words reminded her that it was some time since they had in fact done so. Most of those invigorating outings had taken place in the early days of their marriage. She thought suddenly, Oh Malcolm, you really should have married Barbara – she'd have been much better for you. Did he regret his choice? It was a question she could never ask.

The evening wore on and eventually Jenny looked at her watch. 'We'd better be making a move; the baby-sitter's rates go up at midnight and it'll take us a good half-hour to get home.'

Reluctantly everyone got to their feet. Sally went to collect her three-month-old son from the spare bedroom, returning with him still asleep in his carrycot. 'With luck, we can transfer him to his car-seat without waking him,' she said, looking fondly down on the small, red face.

Una surreptitiously stepped to one side. Young Jamie had a distressing tendency to bawl every time he laid eyes on her, a practice of which his father, judging by the smug expression on his face, heartily approved.

They moved in a body into the hall, coats were sorted out, thank yous and goodbyes said. Malcolm, who had drunk more wine than he was used to, was in mellow mood, and with a sinking heart Una knew how he proposed to end his birthday. Possibly because she'd come to it late, she found the physical side of marriage both ludicrous and embarrassing.

He closed the door on the last of his family and put his arm round her, confirming her fears. 'And now,' he murmured, his breath hot in her ear, 'I have you all to myself.'

'Enjoy yourself?' Tim asked abruptly as they turned on to the Shillingham ring road.

'Yes, it went well, didn't it? I'm glad your dad liked his present.'

'Stepmamma was in good form when she finally turned up. Probably because she'd given someone the sack.'

'Oh darling, that's not fair!'

'She's so bloody sarcastic,' Tim said resentfully. '"Plenty of crowns and other lucrative treatments?"' He savagely mimicked Una's precise accent.

'She was only showing interest.'

'Interest my eye. She hates having us there. That's the only reason I keep going.'

'Tim! What about your father?'

'There are plenty of opportunities of seeing him without trailing out to Lethbridge. Anyway, it doesn't feel like home any more, since that woman revamped it.'

Jenny wisely kept silent. Before her marriage, Una had embarked on what she termed a 'facelift' of the house, which had involved complete redecoration, several pairs of new curtains, and a wholesale reshuffling of furniture.

Some of the pieces she'd dispensed with altogether to make room for her own, infuriating Tim and his sisters, even though they'd acquired the cast-offs. Carol's piano had caused the most upset, but she'd been only a mediocre player who, for years, hadn't touched it at all, whereas Una, like it or not, was a talented pianist. It was natural she should want her own instrument, though none of the others would see it.

Privately, Jenny considered the house much improved by Una's ministrations; not only had she some lovely furniture but she'd an eye for colour and, when all was said, the pale shades which predominated in Carol's time *had* been uninspired. It would be unwise, however, to express this opinion.

'She always asks after the children,' she said now, hoping to divert Tim from his spleen.

'Angling to see them, no doubt, but tonight's duty visit is more than enough to be going on with.'

'They're quite fond of her, you know, and she's very good to them. That toy piano she gave Lisa must have cost a bomb.'

'The oldest trick in the book,' he said scornfully, 'buying her way into their favour. I'm surprised you fell for it.'

17

Jenny gave up and, settling back in her seat, resolved to say no more.

Una did not sleep well that night. The memory of Malcolm's fumbling embrace alternated continuously with scenes from the evening – Barbara's cool voice and Neil's arrogant stare. Those were the two, she reflected, who caused her most disquiet. Barbara was at least civil, but Neil made no attempt to hide his dislike. He was a thoroughly unpleasant young man, and, whether fairly or not, she held him largely to blame for the attitude of the others.

She sighed, wishing she could toss and turn as she longed to, but reluctant to disturb her husband. How had she arrived at this pass? she wondered despairingly, though she knew the answer. Malcolm had thought her solitary air mirrored his own loneliness, thus creating what she now recognized as a false bond between them.

Still, they co-existed amicably enough most of the time, and she *was* fond of him, even if that fondness was mixed with impatient exasperation. If only the family lived farther away, they would have more chance of making a success of their marriage.

At last, uneasily, she slept.

2

When Una woke the next morning, her mind instantly switched to the problem of Pat's replacement. She couldn't simply phone a secretarial bureau; all her girls were hand-picked and proficient in at least four languages. It might be months before she found a suitable candidate. Oh, *blast* the woman – why did she have to be so touchy?

She showered and dressed quickly and ran downstairs. Malcolm, seated with the paper at the kitchen table, was just finishing his breakfast. Since Una had only coffee in the morning, there was no point in his waiting for her.

He pushed back his chair. 'Well, duty calls. What time will you be back this evening?'

'I really don't know,' she answered distractedly. 'There's a rehearsal, so I'll go straight on from work.'

'Back to the TV dinners, eh?' Malcolm commented, but there was no rancour in his voice.

'There are some vegetables left from last night, and half the fruit pie. No duck, I'm afraid – it all went.'

'I'll survive.' He kissed her cheek. 'See you eventually, no doubt.'

Una nodded, pouring her coffee, and moved to the window to drink it, staring unseeingly down the narrow garden, where spring shoots were pushing through the soil and thrushes hopped over the grass. Possibly in the short term they could make do with someone who simply spoke French –

Her deliberations were interrupted by a knock on the back door. She opened it to find a small, sharp-faced woman on the step, and stared at her blankly.

19

'Morning, mum.'

As Una showed no recognition, the woman added awkwardly, 'I'm the new cleaner, like. Mrs Jones.'

'Oh, of course. Forgive me. Come in, Mrs Jones.'

In fact, Una had engaged her herself, some two weeks previously when May had broken the news that her husband's firm was moving him up north. With little interest in domestic affairs, she'd forgotten Friday had been May's last day. Now, watching as Mrs Jones removed her coat to reveal a skinny frame encased in a flowered overall, she wondered if she'd made the right choice. The woman didn't look strong enough to heave furniture about. She was older than May, too, thin-faced, with a sharp nose and mousey hair. But she had spun some hard-luck story – widow, son out of work – and Una, anxious to get to the office, had weakened and agreed to give her a trial.

Quickly she now showed Mrs Jones where the cleaning equipment was kept. 'Tuesdays and Fridays, I think we said? Upstairs one day, downstairs the other. I'll leave your wages on the side on Friday mornings, if that's all right. Now you must excuse me – I'm late as it is. Don't forget to lock up when you go. The front door's on a Yale, so you only have to pull it shut behind you.'

And with an absent-minded smile, Una left her to it.

Malcolm Bennett made a point of always walking to and from the police station. It was virtually no distance, and if he needed a car during working hours, his sergeant was always there to drive him.

Normally, he made use of the ten-minute walk to clear his mind for the day ahead, and many was the problem that had painlessly resolved itself during this interval between home and office.

Today, though, domestic worries persisted and he could see no way round them. He might as well face it, he told himself wearily, his second marriage had been a mistake.

When he and Una had met, both of them relaxed and in holiday mood, they'd got on well together and enjoyed each other's company. Admittedly he'd never felt any deep love for her, but he'd ached for companionship and assumed that she did, too. He'd hoped – confidently expected, in fact – that life together would ease that loneliness for both of them.

But he'd overlooked an important point: for twenty years Una had been a career woman, whose free time was devoted to music – an interest he did not share. It soon became clear she'd no intention of changing her lifestyle to accommodate her marriage, and he'd had to resign himself to the fact with as good a grace as he could muster.

Nor was that the only problem. Having previously enjoyed a satisfying sex life, he'd hoped they would be compatible in that area. They were not. He could almost feel her steeling herself to his touch, submitting to his – God knew – infrequent demands out of an old-fashioned sense of duty. Last night had been a case in point. 'Close your eyes and think of England!' he told himself with grim humour.

Then there were the kids; admittedly he'd remarried too soon, and the old, close relationship with them had still not been restored. But it wasn't just the timing; they obviously disliked Una, which upset him for all their sakes. Powerless to intervene, he could only watch helplessly as they rubbed each other the wrong way. Worse, through some cockeyed feeling of loyalty to Carol, he felt it was the children's 'side' he should be taking rather than his wife's.

If only she'd relax, be more natural, let them get to know her as he had in Scotland. After all, she was bright and interesting and had an unsuspected but astute sense of humour. He guessed that her standoffishness was due to shyness and, despite her successful career, a feeling of insecurity. But it had all been so different with Carol. Oh God, my love, he thought on an agonized wave of grief, why did you have to die?

He had reached the foot of the hill and brushed his hand impatiently across his eyes as he waited for a gap in the rush-hour traffic. And in a moment of rare self-analysis he saw that he'd had another reason for remarrying as soon as possible: he did not want to become a liability to his children. He'd been acutely aware that his bereavement had upset the balance. There was Tim and Jenny, and Sally and Neil, and Jane and

21

Steve. And him. Poor old Dad. Have to ask him along – he must be lonely.

Admittedly, there'd never been the slightest suggestion of anything other than a genuine desire for his company, but it had still been early days and he'd a horror of imposing himself on them, of their feeling they ought, rather than wanted, to invite him to the Sunday lunches which had become a routine after Carol died. Eventually it might even have degenerated into, 'But it's your turn to have him!' Subconsciously, his second marriage had in part been designed to relieve them of responsibility.

Then there was Barbara. Oh God, Barbara! He'd realized too late that they'd all been expecting him to marry her. Had it not been for that coach trip to Scotland, he might well have done, in time. Not that he imagined himself 'in love' with her – how adolescent the phrase sounded! But, he now acknowledged wryly, she'd have fulfilled the position of pleasant, affectionate companion much more comfortably than did Una, and she was already 'family'.

'Cheer up, mate, it might never happen!' said a voice beside him as a hand came down on his shoulder, and, turning, he saw DI Brian Stratton.

He forced a grin. 'Sorry, did I look that bad?'

'Worse! What is it, a birthday hangover?'

'Must be,' Bennett agreed, and, finally shaking himself free of his worries, he turned with Stratton into the familiar entrance of Lethbridge Police Station.

Una drove into the private car park which her office shared with the rest of the building. Parking was at a premium in the centre of Shillingham and they were luckier than most to have this advantage. Having locked the car and set the alarm, she went into the building, along the tiled corridor to the mahogany-doored lifts and up to the second floor where her offices lay.

Even today, with the prospect of a morning spent on the phone to staff agencies, she experienced the usual lift of pride and pleasure as she pushed open the glass door with the inscription *Drew's Translation Services*. Shortly, they'd be celebrating ten years of its existence, and she had decided on an all-round salary increase and a staff dinner at the King's Head.

In the foyer, Rosemary, the receptionist, was on the phone. She nodded smilingly as Una passed. In an all-embracing glance, Una took in the fresh flowers, the pile of new magazines neatly arranged on the low table, the plumped-up cushions of chairs and sofas awaiting prospective clients.

She had designed the layout of the offices herself. To the right of the foyer were three small rooms where foreign businessmen visiting the town could effect their transactions in private with the help of an appropriately speaking secretary. Facing the entrance was the manageress's office and alongside it a short passage leading to Una's own office on the right and, opposite, to the rest-room and small kitchenette. When business was brisk, the girls had the option of bringing their own lunch rather than having to go out for it.

On the left of the foyer was the large general office. Each of the six girls had her own word-processor, printer and telephone, with shared use of the fax and photocopier. All six were proficient in French, German, Spanish and Italian, while one also specialized in Japanese and another – Pat, in fact – in Russian.

Una hung her jacket on the coat rack and walked over to her desk, flicking through the pile of mail which lay, envelopes neatly slit open, awaiting her attention. She moved round behind the desk and had just seated herself when, following a knock on the door, the manageress came in.

Eve Bundy was in her early fifties, a trim, efficient woman with a lifetime spent in office management. Her short, well-styled grey hair and smart suit instilled confidence and she ran her staff firmly but fairly. She also doubled, when need arose, as Una's private secretary.

'I'm sorry to bother you, Miss Drew, but I wonder if you could spare a minute?'

Una had retained her maiden name for business purposes.

'Of course, Mrs Bundy. Come and sit down.'

The woman did so, crossing her slender ankles. 'It's about Pat.'

Una looked up. 'Yes?'

'I had a phone call from her last night. She was very upset. She still is.'

Una said stiffly, 'Mrs Bundy, she handed in her notice. I didn't dismiss her.'

'Yes, I know that.' The woman flushed. 'I wish you'd let me know her last piece of work was unsatisfactory. It might have been easier if I'd dealt with the matter.'

'By which you mean,' Una said drily, 'that you'd have been more tactful.' Mrs Bundy was the only person from whom she'd accept implied criticism. Similar instances had arisen before, when Una's sharp tongue had caused upset or offence and the manageress had had to smooth things over.

Though her flush deepened, Mrs Bundy didn't reply directly. 'Although I'm not making excuses for her, she has been under a strain at home. Her daughter has chronic asthma, and I gather none of them has had a good night's sleep in weeks.'

'I'm sorry to hear it.' Una sat back, tapping her pen on her desk and waiting for the manageress to come to the point. Which she now did.

'The fact is, Miss Drew, she deeply regrets her outburst, apologizes for what she admits was slipshod work, and wonders whether you'd allow her to withdraw her notice.'

Una drew a deep breath of relief. 'In the circumstances,' she said, 'I have no objection.'

Sergeant Jackson put his sandy head round Webb's door.

'Thought you'd want to know, Guv; another shop raid, and more serious this time. Someone's been hurt.'

Webb swore softly. 'Where was it?'

'Patel's the newsagent's, Dick Lane.'

'A racial attack?'

Jackson shrugged. 'Shouldn't think so. More likely opportunist, like the others.'

'And someone's hurt, you say?'

'Mrs Patel, the owner's wife. Don't know the details; Joe Kenworthy phoned in a couple of minutes ago.'

Webb pushed back his chair. 'I'll take a look at this one myself, Ken. I was talking to DCI Bennett from Lethbridge;

they're having the same problem, same MO. Let's see if we can nail them before they do any more damage.'

The previous day's rain had cleared, the sky was high and blue with scudding clouds, and it was possible to believe that spring was after all just round the corner. Even Station Road looked quite pleasant, and after months of scuttling, heads bent, from one shelter to another, shoppers were thronging the pavements in the bright sunshine.

Jackson whistled softly as he turned the car into the narrow entrance of Dick Lane. In this backwater the shouts from the school playground contrasted sharply with the silent group huddled outside the newsagent. A uniformed officer stood in the doorway, keeping them at bay.

Jackson, suddenly sobered, stopped whistling and drew the car into the kerb. Before he'd switched off the ignition Webb had the door open and was striding across the pavement.

The constable straightened. 'If you wouldn't mind going round the back, sir, to preserve the scene – ?'

'Of course.' Webb walked swiftly down the narrow alley alongside the shop, pushed open a gate in the wall and let himself into the back premises.

The interior was dim after the bright morning. A young Asian woman was sitting on a chair clutching her arm, round which a hasty bandage had been wrapped. Her husband stood behind her, one hand on her shoulder, while he tried to answer the police sergeant's questions. Through the door leading to the shop, Webb caught sight of an open cash till and empty shelves.

Thomson broke off as he came into the room. ' 'Morning, sir. An ambulance is on its way, but when they heard it wasn't urgent they said it could be twenty minutes.'

Webb nodded. 'Mr and Mrs Patel? DCI Webb, Shillingham CID. What exactly happened?'

The slightly built Asian moistened his lips. 'Well, as I've been telling the officer here, the morning rush was over and about nine-thirty I came through here as usual for a smoke, leaving my wife in charge. I start work at five every morning,' he added defensively, as though they considered him to blame for his wife's injury.

'I'm sure you'd earned a break, sir.'

Patel nodded gratefully. 'Well, I'd just picked up the paper when I heard a commotion at the front, and my wife cried out. I rushed back and there were these three men. One held a knife against Sharmilla, one was at the till, and the third was sweeping packs of cigarettes off the shelves into a black plastic bag.'

He swallowed, his Adam's apple jerking nervously in his throat. 'Well, of course I shouted and ran forward, and the one with the knife slashed at my wife's arm, yelling that if I made another move, it would be her throat next time.

'And – that was it. It was all over in a minute. The other two ran out, and the one holding my wife dragged her to the door. I thought – I thought for a moment they were taking her with them. Then he suddenly flung her away, dashed out and slammed the door behind him. It's a wonder the glass didn't break,' he ended prosaically.

The girl on the chair made a whimpering sound.

Webb bent down to her. 'Are you all right, ma'am?' She nodded, her eyes full of tears. 'The ambulance shouldn't be long.' He straightened. 'Now, Mr Patel, these men; can you describe them?'

'Not really. They wore woollen helmets, with holes for their eyes.'

'What colour helmets?'

He hesitated. 'Dark green, I think. Yes, green.'

'What else were they wearing?'

'Jeans, leather-type jackets, trainers.'

Yob uniform, Webb thought in frustration, worn, unfortunately, by half the male population.

'Were they tall, short, fat, thin?'

Patel shrugged helplessly. 'Average, that's all I can say.'

'And their voices – any accent?'

'Only one of them spoke. I think he was white, but apart from that –' and he shrugged again.

Perhaps it was optimistic to expect the man to identify an

accent. 'Did you notice which way they went? If they had a car?'

Patel shook his head. 'I was too busy seeing to my wife.'

Webb said reflectively, 'You say you always come through here about nine-thirty. Might they have known that? That your wife would be alone in the shop at that time?'

The man stared at him in horror. 'You think they could be customers?'

'If not, they certainly struck lucky.'

A siren sounded outside, becoming progressively louder, and through the shop door Webb saw an ambulance draw up. The crowd on the pavement parted like the Red Sea, allowing the men through with a stretcher, and a moment later they appeared at the back door.

A swift examination, however, showed the stretcher to be unnecessary, and within minutes the young woman was being led outside.

Patel turned to Webb. 'Sir, have you finished here? I must lock up and go with my wife.'

'Go by all means, but there's no need to lock up; scenes-of-crime officers will be here shortly, and in the meantime PC Kenworthy will remain on guard outside.'

The man hesitated briefly, then hurried after his wife. Webb and Thomson conferred for a moment before following him. By the time they reached the pavement, the crowd, still for the most part silent, was watching the ambulance disappear down the road.

'Did any of you see what happened?' Webb asked them.

They shook their heads. They were mostly women, some middle-aged with shopping baskets, some younger, with babies in prams. But a man at the back spoke up.

'I saw the van arrive,' he volunteered.

'What van?'

'That the robbers got out of. Blue Bedford. Can't remember the number, but it was B-reg.'

Webb's voice quickened with interest. 'So you saw them go into the shop?'

'Not exactly. I just saw it draw up as I turned into my gate.' He nodded at a house across the road. 'But a moment later

27

there was a crash as they slammed the shop door and I ran to the window to see what was going on. That's when I caught a glimpse of the last one getting in.'

'Description?'

'Quite heavily built, wearing jeans and a jacket. He pulled off the helmet as he shut the van door – dark hair, I think, but like I said, I only caught a glimpse.'

'Did you see any of the others?'

'The driver stayed in the van, but from where I was, I could only see his arm and shoulder through the window.'

'You're sure he didn't get out?'

''Course I'm sure; he had the engine running all the time.'

So there were four of them. Webb turned to the intent, listening faces. 'Can anyone add to that?'

A young woman said hesitantly, 'I did see them run out, three of them, but I was quite a way down the road. One was carrying a black bin-bag. The last one flung himself into the back of the van as it was already moving off.'

'Thank you. Anyone else?'

There was no further response.

'Right, well, if you two would give your names and addresses to the officer here, we'll contact you later for statements.'

The young woman looked alarmed. 'I won't have to go to court, will I? I don't want them knowing who I am.' She shuddered.

'I don't think that'll be necessary. All right, ladies and gentlemen, the excitement's over, you can go home now.'

And with a brief nod which encompassed them all, he climbed into the car beside Jackson.

During the afternoon, the report came through on the shop. No fingerprints on the till – the thief had worn woollen gloves – but a few fibres had been lifted from it and the door handle.

They'd had more luck with the floor, though. The pavement had been wet after the previous night's rain, and there was a wealth of blurred foot marks. SOCO had retrieved clear prints of two different shoes which, since they'd been superimposed on the others, had presumably been left by the gang. Both had been made by trainers.

'Until we match up the fibres and the trainers, we're no further on,' Webb commented gloomily. 'Can you think of any villains with this MO, Alan?'

DI Crombie regarded him over the top of his spectacles. 'The only ones that come to mind – Johnnie Harris and his gang – are inside at the moment.'

'Sure? No chance they've been let out early?'

'Not that I've heard.'

'Might be worth phoning the nick to make sure they haven't legged it over the wall.'

'I wouldn't advise it; they're still touchy over that hanging they had.'

'OK, so suppose Harris is in the clear – for this one, at least. Anyone else?'

'There are the Barclay twins, but they've been keeping their noses clean lately.'

'No harm in sending Partridge and Manning round for a chat. What about the snouts? Pussy Barlow still on the ball?'

Crombie wrinkled his nose. The little ex-cat burglar had a peculiarly pungent aroma which tended to cling to the station walls after his visits. 'I'm glad to say I've not seen him lately. I'll have a word with Jones, he's his snout.'

Webb glanced at the reports on his desk. 'House-to-house didn't get us very far. At that time of day, the people living opposite were either out at work or washing up breakfast dishes in the kitchen; not, anyway, staring usefully out of their front windows.'

He reached for his phone. 'I'll just give Malcolm Bennett a bell; we're keeping each other informed on these raids.'

He doodled on his pad till Malcolm's voice came over the line.

'Hi, Malc; how did the family celebrations go?'

'Fine, thanks, though I could do without the aftereffects.'

Webb grinned. 'Well, if you didn't already have a headache, this would give you one: there's been another raid.' Rapidly he apprised him of the details. 'At least we've got fibres – black wool – and the shoe-prints. It's a start. We're doing a check on all B-reg blue Bedfords, but it could well turn out to have been stolen. And that's about it for the moment. Hope your head improves – take a couple of aspirins!'

Bennett smiled bleakly as he put the phone down, then looked up as a tap came on his door and a DC put his head round.

'Someone to see you, Guv. Your son-in-law.'

Bennett frowned. 'Neil? All right, you'd better show him in.'

What the hell did the boy want? he thought irritably. As he'd mentioned to Dave, the headache which had been threatening all day was now bearing down painfully and for once in his life he was clock-watching. All he wanted was to go home, settle back in his own armchair and have forty winks. A sign of age, no doubt – or perhaps just the unaccustomed wine last night.

Even at the best of times, he thought ruefully, Neil was one of the last people he'd want to see. He'd tried to like him, God knows, for Sally's sake and to preserve family harmony, but the boy didn't make it easy. He was still smarting from the barbed comments over dinner about his lunch with Dave.

Neil came into the office looking unusually ill at ease and closed the door carefully behind him. Bennett nodded to the chair opposite his desk and he sat down.

'Now, what's all this about? I've not much time to spare.'

Neil cleared his throat. 'Actually, it's a bit embarrassing.'

Bennett leaned back in his chair and eyed him shrewdly. 'In my experience, when people say that, they're usually after a loan.'

To his surprise, the young man flushed scarlet.

'My God, don't say I've hit the nail on the head?'

'I'm afraid you have, yes.' His eyes fell before his father-in-law's suddenly gimlet gaze. 'I made a rather unwise investment which didn't turn out as expected.'

'Which race was it in?'

Neil's eyes flew to his face. 'Now look –'

'All right, only a stab in the dark. But if you're strapped for cash, why don't you approach your own father?'

The young man's knuckles whitened. 'I did. He couldn't help.'

'So you reckoned that a flush policeman, who can afford to splash out on lunch at the Grill, would be a better bet?'

Neil said in a strangled voice, 'I shouldn't have said that. I apologize. But we really are in a jam, and I –'

'How much are we talking about?'

'Well, my immediate need is for five thousand, but –'

'Five *thousand*? God, I thought you were going to touch me for a couple of hundred!'

'It's only a temporary hitch. In a month or two, everything will have worked itself out.'

'I wish I had a pound for every time I've heard that. So your father won't play ball, eh? Does he know something I don't?'

'He's – helped me out before,' Neil said unwillingly.

'And have you repaid him?'

'Not yet.' The admission was barely audible.

'Then can you give me one sound reason why I should throw good money after bad?'

'For your daughter and grandson?'

Bennett's eyes narrowed. 'It's got nothing to do with them, has it? I'm willing to bet they wouldn't see a penny of anything I gave you now.' He shook his head. 'I'm sorry, Neil, I don't think it's in your best interests. If this has happened before, it's time you learned to use your money more responsibly, and you won't do that if you go bleating to someone every time you get your fingers burned.'

'But I really am desperate, Malcolm! If I don't come up with the money, I stand to lose everything I've put in already. Look – I don't quite know how to say this, but – well – you'll be leaving something to Sally eventually, won't you? If you don't want to lend me the money, how about giving her something on account? I'd pay her back later.'

Bennett gave him a long, hard look, and Neil's own eyes fell. Then the older man said heavily, 'I'm going to pretend I didn't hear that. If you're so desperate, how about selling that flash car of yours? Or that set of golf clubs you're so proud of? Let's face it, you're not exactly destitute. You can raise

31

the money all right if you have to, but it will mean putting yourself out and no doubt losing a bit of face in the process. Which, all things considered, might be no bad thing. Now get out, for God's sake, before I lose my temper completely, and don't ever mention this matter again.'

For a long moment the young man held his gaze defiantly. Then, without a word, he got up and walked out of the room. Bennett sat staring after him. Then, slowly, he lowered his aching head into his hands.

3

Barbara Wood dismissed her class and, having gathered her things together, followed them more slowly down the black-and-white tiled corridor as far as the staff-room. Her last period of the day was a free one, and she was grateful.

She was also grateful that, for the moment at least, she had the room to herself. Dumping her satchel, she made herself a cup of tea and carried it back to the table, where she took out a pile of exercise books and spread them in front of her. It was, as she acknowledged to herself, mere window-dressing in case someone came in; she'd no intention of correcting them.

She sighed, sipping despondently at her tea. This vague depression had been with her all day, and until she could get to the root of it, further work would be unproductive.

So – what was the problem? It obviously stemmed from the previous evening, but she'd thought herself inured by now to stressful visits to her family, so different from the happy times when Carol was alive. Nevertheless, she'd have declined last night's invitation had it not been Malcolm's birthday, but she'd always shared in the celebrations, and felt obscurely that she owed it to Carol to continue doing so.

Not that there'd been much sense of celebration last night. To start with, Malcolm himself had looked tired, the lines round eyes and mouth carved more deeply then usual. But to her anxious query, he'd simply smiled and replied, 'I'm overworked, underpaid and the wrong side of fifty. What could possibly be wrong?'

And, smiling back, she had taken the glass he held out and allowed her concern to be overruled. But matters did not improve, Una's continuing absence causing a level of tension which her eventual appearance failed to ease. She had pleaded pressure of work, but Barbara suspected that the dinner had temporarily slipped her mind, and felt less than welcome in consequence.

But it was not Una's deficiencies that were causing her disquiet. What, then? Something that had been said? Neil had been unpleasant, as usual, but again, he'd no power to upset her. The girls, then? Malcolm himself?

Malcolm; yes, he was the nub of the problem. Her first quick concern had been justified; without acknowledging it at the time, she'd known instinctively that he was unhappy.

Barbara frowned, stirring her cooling tea and wondering what had led to that conviction. Despite the resentments his marriage had caused, he'd always seemed content enough. That had been her one grain of comfort.

Deliberately, assessingly, she conjured him up in her mind – not the familiar figure she'd known so long, but Malcolm as he was last night. And with hindsight it was possible to recall the defeated look in his eyes, the weariness behind his determined jollity. Here, without doubt, was the cause of her low spirits.

He'd been through so much, she thought now; the onset of Carol's multiple sclerosis, her slow deterioration, the pain of her death and resulting loneliness. It was time he had some happiness.

The fact that she'd once hoped he would find it with her, Barbara had long since put behind her. She knew the family had expected them to marry – in fact, Jane, with her total lack of guile, had told her so – but only as the sensible course for two lonely people. The possibility of love had never occurred to them.

Then everything had been overturned by Una's arrival: Una, with her stiff smile and unreadable eyes whom, unaccountably, Malcolm wanted to marry. And who had instantly known what neither Malcolm, bless him, nor any of his family, had ever suspected: that Barbara loved him herself. The knowledge hung between them, unspoken but not to be denied, increasing their mutual hostility.

Was Una at the centre of his misery? She seemed so cold and self-contained – the last person, surely, one could turn to for comfort or companionship – an impression strengthened by last night's comments about their separate lives.

On the other hand, Malcolm's despair might have nothing to do with his wife; perhaps there was a problem at work – what had he said, *overworked and underpaid*? – even financial worries.

Alone in the quiet room, Barbara sat lost in anxiety and indecision. And eventually, out in the corridor, the bell rang for the end of afternoon classes. Listlessly she gathered together the scattered exercise books, replaced them in her satchel, and went home.

Sally was feeding her son, lost in a warm, milky daze from which the sound of the front door jolted her. The baby, sensing her shift of attention, raised his head. He'd had enough for the moment, anyway. She rebuttoned her blouse and lifted him to her shoulder, rubbing his small, woollen-clad back and looking expectantly at the door.

When it remained closed, she called, 'Neil?' and after a minute he came into the room, a glass in his hand. She raised her eyebrows.

'Before you even say hello?'

'I'm in need of it.' He came over, kissed her upturned face and absent-mindedly caressed his son's fluffy head.

Sally stifled a sigh; it looked like being another difficult evening. Neil had been increasingly morose lately and her own temper was beginning to fray. Over the last three years, she'd found that the handsome, ambitious young man she'd married could be childishly petulant when things weren't going his way. It had come as a shock to realize that she was the stronger character, and she resented being continually called on to coax him out of his moods, when he never offered her any support.

'Had a bad day?' she asked dutifully, knowing he'd no interest in her own difficulties – the breakdown of the washing-machine, the baby's refusal to sleep.

'A hell of one,' he confirmed, flinging himself into an armchair.

'Well, it's over now. If you could –'

'Actually, it isn't.'

She looked up. 'What do you mean?'

He tipped back his head and emptied the glass. 'I've something to tell you; I've been to see your father.'

'Dad? Why on earth?'

Neil stared moodily into the fire. 'I thought he might help me out of a tight corner, but I should have known better.'

'Well, can you blame him? I asked you not to stir things last night, but you had to get your little dig in, didn't you? If you wanted his help, you should have been more careful.' Neil's attitude to her family – and theirs to him – was a frequent bone of contention between them.

'Last night,' Neil said heavily, 'I thought I had time in hand. This morning, I found I hadn't.'

'Time for what?'

'To find the money I need to put me in the clear.'

Sally stared at him, suddenly aware that the matter was more serious than she'd supposed. 'What's happened? For God's sake, Neil, what have you done?'

He tilted his glass, rolling the remaining drops round and round the rim. 'It seemed a safe bet at the time, a quick way to make a packet. Damn it, the money was there! It only meant sliding it sideways for a few days.'

Her mouth was dry. Against her shoulder the baby burped gently and turned his head, his warm, wet mouth nuzzling her cheek. She said slowly, 'You gambled with clients' money?'

'Hardly gambled,' he retorted. 'Damn it, there shouldn't have been any risk at all. If it hadn't been for that unexpected drop in the market –'

'And you lost it?'

After a minute he nodded sullenly, not meeting her eyes.

'How much?'

'Not a vast amount; nothing I couldn't –'

'How much, Neil?'

'Around five thousand.'

There was a long pause, then she said tonelessly, 'And you asked Dad for it?'

Another nod.

'What did he say?'

'Wanted to know why I hadn't gone to Father.'

'And why hadn't you?' But she thought she knew the answer. This, she felt instinctively, was not the first time; thinking back, there'd been occasions over the last year or two when their fortunes had seemed to fluctuate, Neil being anxious and withdrawn for a few days, then relieved and confident again. A blip in the market, he'd told her, and she'd probed no further. Now it appeared that Jack Crawford had bailed them out. And refused to do so again, no doubt because the debts were still outstanding.

She said flatly, 'You've borrowed from him before, haven't you?' and took his silence as assent. 'What else did Dad say?'

'Told me to sell the Merc and my clubs. Bloody nerve!'

'Sounds good advice to me. We never needed such a flash car, and you know things have been tight ever since you joined the golf club.'

He said indignantly, 'You seem to forget it was all for your benefit, yours and Jamie's. That's where contacts are made, and if I don't want to miss out, I need to be there.'

'Only if we can afford it, which we obviously can't. So what'll happen? If you can't pay it back in time?'

He stood up abruptly. 'Oh, I'll pay it back, one way or another, but we'll have to remortgage the house and I suppose the Merc will have to go. What it is to have supportive families!' And he went in search of another drink.

The rehearsal had not gone well; one of the soloists had flu, which meant drawing a substitute from the choir, but even allowing for that, the singing was uneven and decidedly below standard. And the concert was only ten days away.

It was therefore later than usual when Una arrived home, and as she turned into the drive she saw that the bedroom light was on. No doubt Malcolm had tired of waiting up for her.

Wearily she let herself into the house and went to the

kitchen to make a hot drink. It had been cold in the church hall, and the hours of singing had dried her throat.

As she waited for the kettle to boil, she saw a note propped against the coffee canister on which was scrawled in an uneducated hand: *We need more floor pollish*. It was signed *R. Jones*.

The new cleaner, who had started this morning. How long ago it seemed. Una spooned chocolate powder into a mug and was pouring on the boiling water when a sound behind her made her turn. Malcolm stood in the doorway in his dressing-gown.

'So you remembered you've a home to go to! Do you know what time it is?'

'To the last second,' she replied, stirring the hot chocolate. 'It was a disastrous rehearsal. Would you like a drink? There's enough water in the kettle.'

He shook his head. 'All I want is to go to sleep.'

'Well, I'm not stopping you.'

'You were, though. You know I can't settle till you're home.'

'For God's sake, Malcolm, I'm not sixteen! I'm perfectly capable of looking after myself. Suppose *I* couldn't settle when you're out on a case? You're often much later than I am.'

'That's different,' he said.

'Why? Because when you're late it's due to work, and when I am, I'm merely enjoying myself?'

'If you want to put it that way,' he said stolidly.

'I don't, but that's how you seem to see it.'

'You're certainly not much company these days.'

'Well, I'm sorry, but if what you want is a docile little wife who stays home all day and has your slippers waiting for you, you've picked the wrong one.'

'Is that a cheap jibe at Carol?' he demanded angrily. 'All right, so she didn't run her own business, or sing in a choir, or any of the other things you're so damn proud of, but she was loyal and loving, and she made a happy home for the kids and me, which is something –'

'– I'm incapable of?' Una broke in, her temper rising to match his. 'And what about my feelings in all this? How do

38

you think I like having to welcome your po-faced family when they come round to sneer at me, knowing I'm continually being compared with the sainted Carol? I –'

She broke off as a sound came from the hallway. Malcolm turned swiftly, putting out his arm as though to hold someone back; but he was too late, and behind him Una saw Jane's pale, startled face.

There was a brittle silence, then Malcolm said flatly, 'I didn't have time to tell you; Jane's spending a few days with us while she sorts out some problems.'

'Oh, *good*!' Una exclaimed, and was instantly ashamed when the girl burst into tears and ran back upstairs.

'Well done,' Malcolm commented.

'What's the matter with her?'

'Had a row with her boyfriend. That's why he wasn't here last night, but she didn't mention it because she didn't want to spoil my birthday. She phoned when I got in this evening.'

'I'm sorry, Malcolm. I shouldn't have flown off the handle like that.'

'Nor should I; I'm sorry, too.'

'If I'd known Jane was here –'

He nodded. 'She probably wondered what all the noise was about.'

'How much do you think she heard?'

He raised his shoulders helplessly.

'I wasn't trying to criticize Carol.'

'I know.'

Una picked up her mug. 'I'll go and have a word with her, tell her she's welcome to stay as long as she likes.'

'Thanks, love.' He turned off the kitchen light and wearily, side by side, they went up to bed.

To Webb's frustration, the rest of the week brought no further progress. There were about a dozen B-registered blue Bedfords in the vicinity, none of which could be linked with the raids. The most likely had belonged to a second-hand car dealer in Station Road, who claimed he'd sold it six weeks previously. His paperwork was sketchy in the extreme, but he assured Partridge that the man who bought it – 'a young lad' – had given the name of Smith. Which, Webb thought disgustedly, was par for the course.

However, on the following Monday things took a more serious turn. When he returned to his office after a meeting, it was to be greeted with the news that there'd been another raid in Lethbridge, and the shop assistant had been seriously injured.

Webb glanced at his watch. It was almost five o'clock and there was nothing urgently awaiting his attention. He decided to clock off early for once and drive over to Lethbridge for an informal chat with Malcolm Bennett.

The road from Shillingham was cross-country, along one of the valleys of the Chantock Hills which bisected the county. It was a pleasant drive on a windy spring day, with lambs in the fields and a wash of new young green along the hedge-rows. Various roads led off to nearby villages – Chedbury, Chipping Claydon, Beckworth – all of which, Webb reflected philosophically, had offered up their share of corpses over the years. And the countryside looked so peaceful!

Steep-gabled farmhouses, woods and roadside stalls of daffodils were interspersed along the way with more prosaic petrol stations and several inviting-looking pubs, most of which Webb could personally vouch for. Eventually the houses became more numerous, the traffic heavier, and he found himself entering the outskirts of Lethbridge.

Like most of Broadshire, the town had changed over the years he'd known it. Old parts still remained, principally around the ancient cobbled marketplace with its stone cross where, every Remembrance Sunday, the local dignitaries laid their wreaths. But several attractive old buildings in the centre had been demolished to make way for what Webb regarded as a horrendous shopping complex. The march of progress, he assumed gloomily.

The police station was on the main road into town, opposite the classically columned Town Hall. Webb turned right on to the open forecourt, grateful that there was just room for his car. It was probably the Super's space, he reflected, but knowing Ray Turner, he'd have gone home by now. Chancing his luck, he locked the car and went up to the steps to the swing doors.

Lethbridge Police Station was not, like Divisional HQ at Shillingham, a modern building. Cramped and dingy, its dim foyer, lined with uninviting wooden benches, always depressed Webb. He approached the duty sergeant and asked for DCI Bennett.

But as he spoke the name, Bennett himself emerged through the security door, his face lighting a little at the sight of Webb.

'Looking for me, Dave?'

'I am indeed. Have you finished for the day?'

'Yes, thank God. Time for a pint?'

'Exactly what I was after.'

'Great; the Roebuck's just round the corner.'

In companionable silence the two men emerged from the building, walked across the concrete forecourt and turned right, following the bend of the road round the corner into the High Street. And, as Bennett had said, came upon the Roebuck public house squatting grey and four-square, its door opening directly off the pavement.

Admittedly it did not look inviting, but Webb had been there before and knew the landlord prided himself on real ale and a high standard of bar food.

It was already filling up as people dropped in for a quick drink after work, and the hum of voices provided a comforting background without, mercifully, the intrusive jangling of piped music. Less acceptably in Webb's view, a fug of cigarette smoke was already building up.

The two men retired to a corner table with their brimming tankards and raised their glasses to each other.

'I suppose you've come about the raid?' Bennett said, wiping the foam from his mouth.

Webb nodded. 'I thought it would be better if you filled me in yourself.'

He could have added, though he did not, that he was glad of the excuse to contact his friend again. Malcolm had been on his mind during the last week, and his appearance now did nothing to allay Webb's uneasiness.

41

'It was an off-licence,' Bennett was saying. 'The manager was out at lunch, leaving a young girl in charge – twenty-two, she is. From what we can gather, it started off as usual – three men barging in wearing balaclavas, and again the knife was in evidence. This time, of course, they were after booze as well as money and fags, and got away with quite a haul. But the girl was brave – or stupid – enough to refuse to open the till. One of the raiders lost his temper, struck out with the knife, and she fell to the floor bleeding heavily. That panicked them. One shouted, "Leave her, Kev!" and they fled.'

'Who gave you that?'

'A couple of kids who were passing. They raised the alarm.'

'Was the blue Bedford in evidence?'

'No such luck. A dirty white Escort, they said, with the driver sitting inside, but everything happened so quickly they didn't get the number.'

'At this rate we'll be looking for all the vans in Broadshire,' Webb said disgustedly. 'How's the girl?'

'Not good; in intensive care.'

'Well, it's hard to know what we can do that we're not already doing, but the press were giving us a bad time even before this. Kev, you said. Do we know anyone of that name?'

Bennett shrugged dispiritedly. 'We've run it through and come up with half a dozen Kevins. No doubt they'll all have cast-iron alibis.'

'If we could find one who has three close pals, it might help. At least it's some lead.'

Bennett nodded, absent-mindedly twisting a ring round and round his little finger. It was a dull green stone flecked with red, in a heavy gold setting. Webb nodded towards it.

'Handsome ring. I noticed it when we had lunch; is it new?'

'My birthday present from Una. Known as a bloodstone, for obvious reasons. Perhaps she thought it went with the job.' He smiled wryly. 'I have to admit I've never considered myself a ring man, but it was a kind thought, and, as you say, it's very handsome.'

Webb came to a quick decision. 'Look, Malc, tell me to take a running jump if you like, but is everything OK? At home, I mean?'

Bennett raised his head slowly and met his eyes. 'We're jogging along, I suppose.'

'But –?'

'Oh God, I don't know. Perhaps we're too alike – pig-headed and used to having our own way. With Carol, I got away with it.'

His voice shook slightly and he took a gulp of beer.

Webb said gently, 'Don't blame yourself if you can't feel for Una what you did for Carol. No one would expect you to. This time, I suppose, you married for – well, affection and companionship.'

'And there's precious little of that.'

Webb was startled at the bitterness in his voice, but before he could comment Bennett went on, 'I feel bloody disloyal, you know, talking about her like this. And I wouldn't, to anyone but you.'

'So what's gone wrong?'

'Nothing spectacular, but – well, she's still as wrapped up in her own pursuits as she was before we married. She's made no concessions whatever.'

'And have you?'

Bennett gave him a startled glance, and after a moment smiled. 'Now that you mention it, probably not. I said we were too alike.'

'Can't you share each other's "pursuits"?'

'I'm not interested in music and she isn't in football.'

'Was Carol?' Webb asked quizzically.

'No, but with her it didn't seem to matter.'

'She was always there when you wanted her, and Una isn't?'

Bennett stared at him for a long minute. 'My God, am I as selfish as that?'

'It's natural enough, but you both need to make allowances.' He grinned in quick embarrassment. 'I sound like an agony aunt!'

'No,' Bennett said seriously, 'you've put it in perspective. We *don't* make allowances, either of us; perhaps that's the root of the trouble.'

'You are still fond of her?'

'Basically, yes.' He gave a twisted smile. 'Specially when I'm not with her; nowadays, it seems that whenever we're together we rub each other the wrong way, and then the fur flies.'

Webb raised an eyebrow. 'She has a temper?' Malcolm's wife had struck him as too cold to warm into anger.

'Hell, yes, she really lets fly sometimes, and so do I. We're both sorry afterwards. There was a case in point last week, and poor Jane landed in the thick of it. She's having problems with the boyfriend – which doesn't surprise me – and asked if she could stay for a few days. Una came in late and the row blew up before I could tell her Jane was there.'

'Is she still with you? Jane, I mean?'

'No, she went back at the weekend. Probably decided the frying pan was better than the fire! I worry about her, though; I don't like this lad she's with and to be honest, I was appalled when she moved in with him. Lord knows what Carol would have thought. But perhaps it's just me being the protective father; I'm not too keen on Sally's husband, either.'

Webb, with no experience of offspring, brought the conversation back to the main problem. 'Didn't you say when we had lunch that Una was in some concert or other?'

'That's right, on Saturday. She has to go over to SB – don't ask me why; they're usually held in Shillingham.'

'How about making a gesture by going along to support her?'

Bennett moved protestingly. 'But she has to be there at two-thirty, for a rehearsal, and it's the big match on telly.'

He caught Webb's eye and laughed shamefacedly. 'All right, you've made your point. I *ought* to make an effort, but not on Saturday, OK? I've been looking forward to this match for weeks.'

Webb shook his head ruefully. 'Confucius, he say, "Good intentions, like diets, always start tomorrow." Seriously, though, you do seem below par, old lad. Are you due for any leave? Take Una and go off for a few days – back to Scotland, perhaps, where you met. That might be a good move – a new start, and all that.'

'Let's get these bloody raids cleared up first.' Bennett

44

drained his glass. 'Now to more cheerful topics: ready for the other half?'

And at Webb's nod, he lifted the two empty tankards and shouldered his way back to the bar.

4

Tuesday morning brought the welcome news that the injured shop assistant, Michelle Taylor, had regained consciousness.

'Go along and see what she remembers, Jeff,' Bennett told his sergeant. 'Debbie Grant's been sitting with her, but she hasn't come up with anything so far.'

Carter nodded. He'd known this would be his job; the governor had been making excuses not to call at the hospital ever since his first wife died there.

'I've been reading the eyewitness accounts,' Bennett was continuing. 'Pretty vague descriptions, when you consider the villains ran right past them.'

'Oh, I don't know, Guv; I'd say it's a wonder they remembered that much. They were terrified, poor kids. Anyway, there's not a lot you can say about blokes in balaclavas.'

'I suppose not. I wonder if it's coincidence that the last two raids took place when the manager wasn't there?'

'Done their homework, more like. Probably it was this bloke's usual lunch break, and Shillingham say the newsagent always went for a smoke when the first rush was over.'

'Well, I'm going to the off-licence now. Meet me at the Roebuck at one, and we can compare notes.'

The shop was on a corner site, and Highbury Street, in which the getaway car had been parked, led directly to one of the main roads out of town – an advantage which had probably not been overlooked.

The shelves, Bennett noted as he pushed open the door, had been restocked, and there was no indication there had been a raid except, perhaps, in the wary stance of the young man behind the counter.

'Mr Braithwaite?' Bennett held up his warrant card, and the man relaxed. Then, almost immediately, concern flooded his face.

'Have you come about Michelle? She's not –?'

'Miss Taylor is making good progress,' Bennett assured him. 'She's regained consciousness and my sergeant has gone to the hospital to take a statement.'

'Thank God! Are you any nearer finding out who did it?'

'I'm hoping you might help us on that one.'

'Me? But I wasn't even here! Didn't they tell you –?'

'Where exactly were you, Mr Braithwaite?'

'It was my lunch break and I'd slipped home. I don't normally, but my wife's expecting a baby any minute and I wanted to check she was OK.'

'And where's home?'

'Netherby Lane, up past the church. I left here spot on twelve and was home by ten-past. I didn't know anything about the raid till I got back just after one and found police everywhere.'

'Do you always take your lunch break at that time?'

'No, usually Michelle goes from twelve to one, and I have one to two. But yesterday my wife was going to the clinic, so we swopped round.'

If the thieves hadn't planned for Braithwaite's absence, they might have just struck lucky in Shillingham, too. Though even if the men had been there, it wouldn't have made much difference. There was little they could have done when threatened with a knife.

'Have you noticed anyone hanging around lately?' he asked. 'Any customers making a nuisance of themselves?'

'Not really. We often get groups of lads in for beer and cigarettes, and they kid Michelle along – ask her out and so on – but they don't really cause trouble.'

'No one took offence when she refused to go out with him?'

Braithwaite looked startled. 'I don't think so. You mean it could be a personal attack?'

47

'We're keeping our options open, that's all. Has the shop been robbed before?'

'Not that I know of. Certainly not while I've been here, which is getting on for three years now.'

'Very well, Mr Braithwaite, thanks for your help. If you think of anything that might be useful, you can get me at the police station. And I hope all goes well with your wife.'

The young man smiled for the first time. 'Thank you,' he said.

Bennett stood for a moment on the pavement outside, looking up and down the road. The entrance to the shop was on Malvern Road, which finished in a T-junction at either end, one giving on to the High Street and the other, Barnaby Lane. It was long and fairly narrow, with what he considered second-class shops jostling one against the other.

Those opposite the off-licence were a small sub-post office, an Indian grocer's and an electrical repair shop. Judging by the lopsided curtains in the windows above, their owners lived over the shops. They had, of course, been interviewed the previous afternoon, but all professed to have seen nothing, and since their own shop windows were stacked high with goods, it was quite possible they were telling the truth.

Bennett moved to the corner and stood with his hands in his pockets, staring down Highbury Street to the Ashmartin Road. Here, there were a couple of estate agent's, a stationery shop with photocopying facilities, several blocks of offices and, nearer the main road, a garage and filling station. Again, no one admitted seeing anything. Talk about the wise monkeys, he thought in frustration. But to be fair, unless someone had spotted the three men actually running out of the shop – which had taken less than a minute – nothing about the parked van would have aroused suspicion.

So where were they based, this gang of four – Shillingham, or here in Lethbridge? It was anyone's guess. He wondered how Jeff was getting on at the hospital. One of these days, he told himself, he'd have to go there himself. It was nearly three years since Carol had died, and he couldn't run away from painful memories all his life. Anyway, they were locked in his head, not in the long, antiseptic corridors of the hospital.

48

He sighed and, stuffing his hands still further into his pockets, started to walk back towards the High Street.

Barbara's little house was situated in a quiet road near the park, within easy walking distance of Ashbourne School. Carol had called it a doll's house, but what did she want with anything larger? She had spent time and money on it over the years, and it now suited her to perfection.

She'd stayed on at school that Tuesday for extra coaching, and it was dusk by the time she arrived home. But as always she felt a lift of the spirits as she turned into the small, paved garden with its sundial and pots of shrubs and spring flowers. The house itself boasted a porch with an outer door – grandly referred to by the estate agent as a 'vestibule' – and Barbara smiled at the pretension as she unlocked both doors and let herself into the small, narrow hall with its white walls and leaf-green carpet.

Originally, there'd been two small rooms off to the left, which, after some thought, she'd had knocked into one. It was still not large, but Barbara loved it and, having hung her coat on the hall stand, she went in to switch on the lamps, delighting in the soft lights that sprang up, one after another, to shine on her treasured possessions.

There was a window at each end of the room, draped with flamingo-pink curtains suspended from wooden poles. Their sharp colour, echoed by cushions on the chairs, contrasted strikingly with the muted tones of the rest of the room. Barbara seldom drew the curtains, preferring merely to pull down blinds to shield the lighted room from passers-by.

At the back window, she paused as she always did to look out at the small, walled garden, merging now into darkness. The lawn, she noted, was just about ready for its first cut of the season.

Turning away, her thoughts moved to the more immediate prospect of supper. There was a chicken casserole in the fridge, and she decided to open a bottle of wine. If she vacuum-sealed it, it would last for several days, adding pleasure to whatever mundane fare she happened to be eating.

She went through to the tiny kitchen at the end of the hall, where everything was within arm's reach, and had just lit the oven when the doorbell rang. She straightened, frowning. She wasn't expecting anyone, and was in no mood to deal with on-spec double-glazing salesmen. She walked quickly back up the hall, flung open the porch door and, to her surprise, found Jane standing on the step.

For a moment, she wondered wildly whether she'd issued an invitation which she had since forgotten. But Jane was saying quickly, 'I'm sorry to drop in out of the blue. Is it very inconvenient?'

'Of course not, dear, I've not been back long myself. Go into the sitting-room; I shan't be a moment – I was just putting a casserole in the oven.'

When, minutes later, Barbara joined her, Jane was standing by the marble fireplace, studying the family photographs which hung beside the mirror. She turned as her aunt came in, her eyes moving appreciatively over the deep sofas and easy chairs, the lamps strategically placed on small tables, the exquisite Indian rug on the deep-piled carpet.

'This is my very favourite room,' she said. 'Just walking into it makes you feel better.'

'I'm glad to hear it, because that was my intention.'

'Everything's so – *comfortable*!'

Barbara smiled. 'Well, I decided that since I spend my days on hard chairs in austere classrooms, I deserve a little luxury at home. Now, can I offer you a drink?'

'Have you any beer?'

'I'm afraid not, but I've just opened a bottle of wine.'

'That'd be fine.'

Jane settled herself on one of the sofas, wriggling into its soft cushions like a puppy and, having handed her her glass, Barbara also sat down.

'Now, to what do I owe this pleasure?'

The girl took a gulp of wine. She looked very young, Barbara thought, with her shaggy curls and Carol's large grey eyes, but then she wasn't much older than the pupils she'd just left.

Jane looked up, meeting her gaze. 'Have you spoken to Dad recently?'

50

'Not since the birthday party. Why?'

'I turned up on his doorstep, too – I wondered if he'd mentioned it. In fact, I spent two or three nights there.'

'Oh? Why was that?'

The girl's eyes dropped. 'Things aren't too good with Steve at the moment. I wanted to get away for a bit, talk it over with someone.'

'And did you? Talk it over, I mean?'

Jane shook her head. 'Dad's got enough problems of his own, and Una – well, she's not the kind you confide in, is she?'

All Barbara's anxieties surged back. She said carefully, 'What do you mean, your father has enough problems?'

Jane flushed. 'Nothing in particular.'

Barbara studied her niece's closed face. This was her favourite of Carol's children, though she tried not to show it, and it seemed that worry about her father was adding to her other problems.

'Jane?' she prompted gently.

'I shouldn't have said anything, but – well, Una and Dad had a row the night I arrived. I heard them shouting at each other and went downstairs. I know I shouldn't have, but I was half asleep and didn't know what was happening. So that made things awkward right at the start, and though Una was quite nice about it and said I could stay as long as I liked, I could tell she didn't really want me to.'

Barbara knew she shouldn't ask, but was unable to stop herself. 'What was the row about?'

'Oh, Dad said she wasn't much company, and she called Mummy "the sainted Carol" and the rest of us "po-faced". It was pretty unpleasant.'

'It must have been,' Barbara said quietly. 'But you know, people can have rows and still love each other.' It cost her something to say that.

Jane merely nodded, rubbing a finger round the rim of her glass.

'Does that auntish comment help you and Steve?'

'Not really; our row was different.'

'Do you still want to talk about it?'

Jane looked up. 'Would you mind?'

'Of course I wouldn't.'

'You see, I don't know what to do. I think I still love Steve, but I hate what he's doing. That's what the row was about; he wanted to know if I was going to shop him to Dad.'

'*Shop* him?' Barbara repeated sharply. 'You mean he's doing something illegal?'

Miserably, Jane nodded. 'He didn't want me to know – because of Dad being in the police, I suppose. But we went out for a drink with Tony, who works with him, and his girlfriend, and Tony let it slip. He didn't realize Steve hadn't told me.'

'So what is it they're up to?'

'You know he works at Savemore in Duke Street?'

'Yes?'

'Well, he and Tony fill the shelves, and I think they've got some scheme going, creaming off items of stock. I don't know the details.'

'I see,' Barbara said – inadequately, she felt.

'Anyway, Tony made a joke about lining their pockets and Steve was furious. When we got home I asked him about it, and he said he was doing it for us, because neither of us earns much and we need more money. I said I didn't want it if that was the way he got it, and he said I was a prissy little cow who didn't know what life was about.'

Jane fished in her pocket for a handkerchief and blew her nose.

After a moment, Barbara said, 'If you *had* talked to your father, would you have told him what Steve was doing?'

'Oh no, only the rows and things, but after hearing him and Una, I didn't feel I could.' She added bleakly, 'He's never liked Steve anyway.'

Barbara thought of the brash, rather aggressive young man, remembering her distress when Jane had moved into his dreary little flat in Dick Lane.

'Even if I had told Dad,' Jane went on, 'he couldn't have done anything, could he, without some sort of proof?'

'It's a delicate area, I agree. I suppose he could have put the store manager on his guard.'

'But think how I'd feel if Steve and Tony went to prison because of me.'

'Anyway, you went back to him.'

'Yes, but things are even worse. He wouldn't believe I'd not said anything, and I began to wish I had. I told him if he didn't stop, I would.'

'Blackmail? Oh, Jane!'

'I know. And the worst thing is I can't trust him any more. Even if he *says* he's doing nothing wrong, I won't believe him.' She looked at her aunt beseechingly. 'What do you think I should do?'

'It sounds to me as though you've already decided.'

'But what do *you* think?'

'As you said, now you're aware of his dishonesty, it will be very difficult, specially when you're with your father, having to watch what you say all the time. And if you ever mislay any money, or a piece of jewellery, you'll immediately wonder if he's taken it.'

Jane nodded, her eyes filling with tears. 'Yes. I know you're right, and part of me agrees with you. The trouble is, the other part still loves him.'

Barbara moved quickly to the sofa and put an arm round her. 'I'm so sorry, darling. How miserable for you.'

For several minutes, Jane leant against her, sniffing from time to time. Then she sat up and blew her nose again. 'Right, that's settled then, and the sooner it's over, the better.'

'You'll move out straight away? Where will you go?'

Jane gave a watery smile. 'It's funny how things work out. I met Emma for lunch today – my best friend from school, remember?'

Barbara nodded, recalling a small child with pigtails.

'She's been sharing a house in Oakacre with a girl who's just left to get married. She asked if I'd like to go in with her.'

Barbara drew a sigh of relief. 'That would be an excellent solution.' And Oakacre, she thought, was a much nicer neighbourhood than Dick Lane, where they'd had that raid only last week.

'Now, would you like to stay for supper?'

Jane wiped her eyes. 'I'd love to. It smells wonderful.'

'Then I'll see to the vegetables while you lay the table. It won't need opening out for just the two of us.'

It seemed that Jane's problems were on the way to being solved, Barbara thought thankfully as she put a light under the potatoes; but Malcolm and Una's might prove a little more difficult.

The letter box rattled as Una came downstairs on the Friday morning, and she collected the envelopes from the mat and carried them into the kitchen, dropping those addressed to Malcolm on the table beside him.

He picked up a hand-written one, frowning. 'This is from Jane. Whatever's she writing about?' He tore open the envelope and ran his eyes swiftly down the single sheet of paper.

'Well, well,' he said slowly. 'She's leaving Steve.'

'Thank goodness for that.'

'But why didn't she say anything while she was here?'

'She mightn't have made up her mind then.'

'All the same, you'd think she'd have phoned, rather than write.'

'Perhaps it's not easy for her to talk about,' Una suggested.

'Yes, that'll be it. Poor kid. Anyway, this is ostensibly to give us her new address and phone number. She's moving into Oakacre this weekend, to join a schoolfriend. I must say, it's a relief. I never did take to that boy.'

He laid the sheet aside and went on with his breakfast, glancing through the rest of his mail as he did so. Una had just poured a second cup of coffee when there was a tentative tap on the back door and Mrs Jones's frizzy head appeared round it.

'Am I too early? The bus before my usual was running late, so I got on that one.' She caught sight of Malcolm and stopped in the doorway. 'Oh, I'm sorry, I'll come back in a few minutes.'

'No, it's all right,' Una told her. 'We won't be long, if you could make a start on one of the other rooms. The new tin of polish is on the side.'

The woman nodded, collected her dusters and the polish and went through to the hall. Malcolm finished his coffee and stood up.

'What are the arrangements for tomorrow, by the way? Will you be here for lunch?'

'No, I've a hair appointment in Shillingham at eleven, so it's not worth coming back. I'll have a sandwich and probably go on the coach with the others; it saves the hassle of driving. What are your plans?'

'I'll look in at the station for a while, but short of a major disaster I'll be back by two, for the build-up to the match.' He paused, remembering Dave's suggestion. 'You don't mind me not coming to the concert, do you?'

She looked at him in surprise. 'You've *never* been to a concert!'

'That's what I mean.'

'What brought this on?'

He said awkwardly, 'Well, I complain about you always being out, but I never make any effort to go with you.'

She gave a short laugh. 'Don't worry about it. Just as long as I don't have to sit and watch football matches!'

Malcolm laughed and, on impulse, bent and kissed her cheek. 'See you later, then.'

He was whistling as he set off down the hill towards the town. Perhaps things weren't so bad after all.

In the event, Una had to modify her plans. As she was sitting under the drier the next morning, she remembered, to her dismay, that she hadn't taken her blouse out of the airing-cupboard.

For a concert away from Shillingham, the choir took the clothes for the performance with them and changed at the hall. The previous evening she had packed the long, burgundy crepe skirt and patent shoes in the small case she kept for such occasions, but had noticed a mark on the blouse, which she'd sponged away. It was then too damp to pack, and she'd meant to collect it from the airing-cupboard in the morning. And forgotten.

Damn! she thought. That meant she'd have to trail back to

Lethbridge after all, and use her own car to go to Steeple Bayliss. Even cutting cross-country it was a good hour's drive, and it would take her half an hour to get home in the first place, specially with the Saturday traffic. And she *hated* rushing before a concert.

It was a quarter to one when she reached the house. She let herself in and ran straight upstairs to the airing-cupboard, removed the blouse, still on its hanger, and ran back down again. In the hall she paused suddenly, aware of an uncomfortable sensation of not being alone.

'Malcolm?' she called sharply. 'Are you there?'

But there was no reply.

It was a nightmare journey; she was behind a tractor all the way to Chipping Claydon, with no means of overtaking it on the twisting country roads. Between there and Marlton she became caught up with a cycle race, which involved being flagged down every now and again by officious stewards to let the competitors pass. And finally, when she reached the main road to Steeple Bayliss, it was to discover two separate lots of roadworks, each with a set of traffic lights.

By this time, hot with frustration, she was feeling decidedly panicky. Keep your mind on the music, she told herself forcibly, blot out everything else.

When at last she reached the town, she'd barely time to swallow a cup of coffee and a sandwich before hurrying to the hall for the rehearsal, where she was greeted with relief.

'We wondered what had happened to you,' Margaret Pearson said. 'I thought you were coming on the coach?'

'So I was, till I discovered I'd left my blouse at home.'

There were exclamations of sympathy.

'Are you all right?' Margaret asked, eyeing her anxiously. 'You look rather – harassed.'

'You'd be harassed,' Una assured her tartly, 'if you'd had the journey I've had.'

'Well, you can relax now – you made it in time.'

'Only just,' Una commented, nodding towards the door as

56

the conductor came into the hall. Abandoning their chat, they all made their way on to the stage.

Normally, Barbara enjoyed her weekends. Sometimes she deliberately left them free, to unwind in pleasant idleness. At others, jealous of her meagre free time, she went to the opposite extreme and planned them in detail: jobs to do, letters to write, articles to read, so that no moment should be wasted. Occasionally she went shopping, or to the theatre with a friend.

But that particular Saturday she was restless, and although there were plenty of things to do, she'd not been able to settle to any of them.

Standing aimlessly at the kitchen window, she thought about Jane, wondering how Steve had reacted to her decision to move out. By now, she should be unpacking her possessions at her new home.

Beyond the glass, the garden lay bathed in afternoon sunshine. Several bushes were waiting to be trimmed, the roses needed pruning and the grass should be dry enough to cut. Yet none of these tasks inspired her to change into her gardening clothes and go outside. The depression that had swamped her after the birthday dinner had returned, fuelled by news of the row Jane had witnessed.

Was there anything she could do to help? Might Malcolm, like his daughter, be glad of a sympathetic ear? She wondered what he was doing, then remembered it was today that Una was singing in Steeple Bayliss. So he'd be alone again.

She looked at her watch, an idea beginning to form. Four o'clock; he was probably home. She'd ring and invite him round to supper; make it casual – say she'd remembered Una was out and wondered if he'd like some company.

With a sense of purpose at last, she hurried to the phone and dialled his number. But it rang and rang unanswered and at last, trying to swallow her disappointment, she replaced the receiver.

*   *   *

The concert had been a great success, playing to a packed, enthusiastic audience. Bowing with the others yet again to continuing applause, Una thought exultantly that it had all been worthwhile – the snatched meals, the hours of rehearsing, the strains and tensions. All were forgotten now in the incomparable thrill of superb music, soaring voices and the rapt audience. Even more importantly, here, part of the large choir tightly packed on stage, she was for once not an outsider.

Caught up in the general euphoria, she wished passionately that the evening could go on for ever, that she need never leave the crowded stage and the flushed, smiling people around her. But eventually the applause died away and, tired but triumphant, they collected their things together for the journey home. Una wished she could climb into the coach with them, extend for a little longer the sense of companionship and enjoy the luxury of being transported home without any effort on her part. Instead, she must face the long, lonely drive across the dark fields, with only her thoughts for company.

It was almost nine-thirty by the time she'd extricated herself from the car park and reached the main road. Briefly, she considered staying on it as far as Shillingham and driving to Lethbridge from there; but despite the better roads, it would add a good twenty minutes to the journey and she dismissed the idea. Better to turn off at Marlton and return the way she had come.

Once or twice, though, she questioned the wisdom of the decision. The main road was well lit and there would have been the company of other traffic. Here, hedges boxed her in and only an occasional lighted farmhouse gave proof of human habitation.

After the tensions of the day and the heat and noise of the hall, a headache was developing, not helped by the concentration of night-driving. She found herself longing for bed and the oblivion of sleep.

But here at last were the outskirts of Lethbridge. The Marlton road entered the town just above the church, on Crossley Hill. She had only to drive down a few hundred yards, turn left into Westwood Avenue, and she was home.

The house as she turned into the driveway was in complete darkness, without the usual light to welcome her. Una sat for a moment, staring up at its black shape looming in front of her. Then she picked up her case and handbag, got out of the car and locked it. The night was very still, but in the distance she heard the braying of an ambulance as it sped up the hill towards the hospital.

Still she hesitated, aware of a strong reluctance to go inside. Then, bracing herself, she put her key in the door and let herself in.

The darkness was absolute, no light showing under any of the doors, and, in its palpable obscurity, the sudden sound of voices set her heart clattering. It took her a moment to realize it was the television.

Quickly she crossed the hall and pushed open the sitting-room door. Here, the darkness was partly alleviated by the flickering light from the set and a shaft of moonlight pouring through the uncurtained windows.

She reached urgently for the switch and light flooded the room, blinding her night-attuned eyes. Malcolm was in his chair opposite the television, his back to the door. She said stridently, involuntarily, 'Malcolm?'

He did not reply, did not, as on previous occasions, wake with a start and turn apologetically to face her. A creeping sensation crawled over her skin and up into her hair. Slowly, giving his chair a wide berth, she moved round it until she could see him properly.

He was slumped sideways, his head sunk on his chest, but she knew sickly that he was not asleep. Knew, because of the dark stickiness matting his hair and the gash above his temple from which, hours earlier, blood had gushed and later caked, leaving a brownish trail down the side of his face and on to his sweater.

Una's eyes stretched wide as the scene burned itself into her brain, forcing her to accept it. He was dead. Her husband was dead. Steeling herself, she approached him and felt

59

the flaccid wrist. It was cold and there was, of course, no pulse.

Behind her, a piercing scream rang out, shattering the silence. Her heart leaping to her throat, she stumbled over and switched off the set.

5

'*Malcolm* Bennett?' Webb said, stunned disbelief in his voice.

'I know; I can't believe it myself.' Superintendent Turner's own voice vibrated with shock. 'I'm sorry, Dave, I know you both go back a long way.'

'But – how? Where?'

'At home. He'd been coshed over the head. Been dead some time, apparently. His wife found him – she's been out all evening. She phoned the station and of course I was notified at once. I got on to the ACC and he'd like you to take charge of the investigation.'

'Of course. I'll go over at once.'

'See you there,' Ray Turner said, and put down the phone.

Hannah appeared in the sitting-room doorway. 'Bad news?' she asked anxiously.

'The worst. Malcolm Bennett's dead. Under suspicious circumstances, at that.'

Hannah's eyes widened. 'The man you met for lunch? Who remarried and – ?'

'The same,' Webb returned grimly.

She came quickly forward and took his hand. 'Oh, David, I'm so sorry. How awful for you.'

'Worse for Malcolm. I've got to go, love.'

'Of course.'

Leaving her standing in the hall, he let himself out of her flat and went clattering down the stairs.

As long as he lived, Webb would never forget that drive to Lethbridge along the road which, so recently, he'd driven to meet Malcolm. Now, he was going to see him again – for the last time. It was impossible to believe, impossible that a friend of such long-standing was suddenly no longer there.

He might have accepted a heart attack, Webb told himself – even a traffic accident. Those things happen. But murder – and, despite official caution, it was almost certainly that – was totally unthinkable. In the early days, he and Malcolm had attended many murder scenes together. Now, irony of ironies, Malcolm was himself the victim.

Policemen had been killed before, God knew, but usually as they went about their duty. To be brutally attacked in his own home was altogether different.

Grimly, methodically, Webb prepared himself for what lay ahead, forcing down the personal loss to make way for a cold, balanced professionalism. And gradually, beneath the shock and grief, a deep, implacable anger began to grow. He welcomed it. It would make things easier.

He hadn't been to the Bennett house since Carol died, and as he drew up behind a row of cars, Webb was fleetingly grateful that at least she had been spared this. Having identified himself to the man at the gate, he went swiftly up the path and into the house, keeping to the prescribed area leading to the sitting-room. Ray Turner met him at the door, his face white and strained above his dark uniform. He put a quick hand on Webb's arm.

'OK, Dave?'

From which Webb gathered his own face mirrored the superintendent's. He nodded briskly. 'So, what have we got?'

Over Turner's shoulder he could see the flashing of cameras as the SOCO photographer moved round the body, and momentarily closed his mind to the object of his attention.

'It's been made to look like a break-in.'

'Made to?' Webb repeated sharply.

Turner raised his shoulders. 'Pane broken in the back door. No tape or anything. It would have made the hell of a din, yet apparently Malcolm didn't hear it and the killer was able to creep up on him and club him to death. His wife says the television was on, but even so –'

The television. Oh God, the match Malcolm had been so

keen not to miss. Ridiculously, Webb found himself hoping he'd been able to see at least a part of it. 'Any lead on time of death?'

'The doc says roughly nine hours ago – early afternoon, I suppose, but of course that's only approximate. We'll have a better idea after the PM. At least there's no doubt about the murder weapon – it's that heavy stick over there. Presumably the killer brought it with him. He used it to break the glass, too, before discarding it: there are splinters among the blood and hair.'

Turner glanced at Webb's wooden face and paused. Then he went on: 'There's been some vandalism, too. Photographs, ornaments and suchlike thrown on the floor and stamped on.'

'You say his wife found him? Where is she?'

'In a car outside with WDC Grant. I'd hoped she might be friendly with another officer's wife and could go there, but it seems she doesn't know anyone.'

'She keeps herself to herself,' Webb said levelly.

'So it appears. Trouble is, the relatives are a bit spread out – son in Frecklemarsh, one daughter in Chedbury, the other God knows where.'

Webb frowned. 'How do you mean?'

'According to Mrs Bennett, they heard yesterday that she'd moved out of her boyfriend's flat, but she can't remember where she's gone. Malcolm had the letter, but so far we haven't unearthed it.'

'They've been informed, the other two?'

'The local police are dealing with it. But when we asked Mrs Bennett who she'd like to go to, she said she'd rather be alone. Can you believe it?'

'I can, actually. They're not *her* family, after all, and they've never been particularly friendly towards her.'

'I see. Poor Malcolm.'

'There must be –'

Beside them the telephone shrilled, making both men jump. Turner took out a handkerchief and used it to lift the receiver.

'Yes?'

A hesitant voice came over the wire. 'Is that the police?'

'Yes, Superintendent Turner speaking. Who's that?' He motioned Webb to come closer.

'Barbara Wood, DCI Bennett's sister-in-law. My nephew has just telephoned with the – the news.'

'I'm very sorry, Mrs Wood.'

'*Miss* Wood,' she corrected him. There was a pause while she steadied her voice. Then she said, 'I was wondering where Mrs Bennett is?'

'At the moment she's with a woman officer. Frankly, we have a bit of a problem; she doesn't want to go to any of her stepchildren.'

'That's why I'm phoning: she must come to me. In any case, I'm the nearest – thirty-three, Coombes Crescent, Shillingham.'

'That's very good of you, Miss Wood.'

'It's what Malcolm would have wanted. I'll make up the spare bed.'

Turner said tentatively, 'There's just a possibility –'

'If she refuses to come, let me know. Otherwise, I'll expect her shortly.'

The last few words were spoken in a rush, and the phone went dead. Control running out, apparently. God, what a business it was.

'Shall I go and have a word with Una?' Webb offered. 'I have met her, with Malcolm.'

'Thanks, Dave. If she's agreeable, Miss Grant can take her straight there; we don't need her any more tonight.'

As he walked down the path, Webb realized for the first time that he had no coat. He'd run straight out from Hannah's flat without bothering to return to his own for outdoor clothes. Now, he was belatedly aware of the coldness of the night, accentuated, no doubt, by his continuing state of shock.

He approached the first car, in which he could make out two figures, and tapped on the glass. A young woman leaned across her companion to open the door.

'DCI Webb, Shillingham.' His eyes went to Una's motionless figure. She sat stiff and straight and hadn't even turned her head in his direction.

'Mrs Bennett – Una – it's David Webb. We've met a couple of times.'

'I remember.' Her voice was low but firm.

'I'm so very sorry about Malcolm. It just doesn't seem possible.'

She inclined her head, still not looking at him.

He cleared his throat. 'Miss Wood's just phoned. She'd like you to go and stay with her till you can get back in the house again.'

'Barbara?' She did turn then, her face a pale disc in the half-light. 'I can't possibly go to *Barbara*.'

'Una, you must go somewhere. You can't sit here all night.'

'But I'll be going back inside soon.'

'Not for a while, I'm afraid. It could take four or five days before –'

'*Days*? But I thought they'd done all their photographing and everything?'

'They'll make a much more thorough examination in daylight. It could take a long time.'

She thought for a moment. 'You're sure it was Barbara who phoned? You didn't ring her?'

'No, she contacted us.'

'And it was she who made the offer? No one asked if I could go to her?'

'No,' Webb repeated patiently, 'it was her own idea. It was the reason she rang.'

Another pause. Then, 'Very well, I suppose I'll have to.'

Over her head, Webb caught the young policewoman's raised eyebrows. He said, 'Miss Grant, perhaps you'd help Mrs Bennett to pack a few things and then take her to thirty-three, Coombes Crescent, Shillingham. Miss Wood will be expecting you.' He turned back to Una. 'Have you something to help you sleep?'

'The doctor gave me some pills.'

'Fine. I'll call round and see you in the morning.'

Slapping his arms for warmth, he hurried back up the path and this time forced himself to go into the room where his friend lay. For several long minutes he stood looking down at the bloodstained white face, the slack mouth. Don't worry, old mate, he thought silently, we'll get the bastard, whoever he is.

He was about to turn away when he paused, glancing back at the dead man's hands. 'Where's his ring?' he asked one of the SOCOs.

'Wasn't wearing one, Guv. Should he have been?'

'He was earlier in the week, one with a green stone.'

'Well, several things are missing, Mrs Bennett says. The killer must have taken it.'

Without replying, Webb turned and walked out of the room.

Barbara must have been watching for the police car, because the door opened as they went up the path, spilling welcome light into the darkness. To Debbie Grant's relief, the two women greeted each other calmly, Mrs Bennett saying simply, 'This is good of you, Barbara.' They were the first words she'd spoken for some time. Thankfully, Debbie released her charge.

'The DCI will be in to see you tomorrow, Mrs Bennett. I hope you manage to sleep.'

'Thank you.'

The suitcase was handed over, the policewoman went back down the path and Una allowed herself to be led into the house. It was warm and dimly lit and she dutifully handed over her coat. It was the first time she'd removed it since she'd put it on in Steeple Bayliss, in another existence. Barbara, she noted dispassionately, was shaking, though her voice was steady.

'Can I get you a drink? Whisky or brandy or something?'

'I'd better not, thank you; I've been given sleeping pills.'

'Of course – I should have thought. A hot drink, then?'

'Tea would be wonderful.'

Barbara hurried out to make it and Una stood in the middle of the room, looking about her. She'd been here only a couple of times, in the early days of her marriage, and remembered little about it. They'd had dinner, she recalled, glancing towards the back of the room where a small, gate-legged table stood, bearing a vase of daffodils. Presumably it opened out for social occasions.

A fire was burning in the grate and a basket of logs stood on the hearth. Una moved over to it, holding out her chilled hands to its warmth. The fact that she was here, in the middle of the night in Barbara's house, only added to the unreality. It was all a dream, and sometime soon she would wake up. It couldn't be soon enough.

She was still standing there when Barbara came back with the tea-tray.

'I love the open fire,' Barbara said, 'though, since I'm out all week, I light it only at weekends.'

Una watched her pour the tea and Barbara glanced up at her. 'Perhaps you'd like to sit down?'

It took a conscious effort to do so, but her hands as she took the cup and saucer were steadier than Barbara's.

'I – don't know if you want to talk about it?'

'There's nothing to say, except what you must already know. I was out at the concert, and when I arrived home I found him.' She drank the entire cup of scalding liquid.

'Tim said there'd been a break-in?'

'Yes; glass all over the floor, and several things missing. I don't know how many – they won't let me look till they've checked for prints.'

'Do they know when – ?'

'They haven't said, but it must have been hours ago. The – the blood was dry.'

Barbara's hand went to her mouth. 'I tried to phone him,' she said after a minute. 'Perhaps he was already – '

Una's head snapped up. 'Oh?'

An explanation seemed called for. 'I remembered you were out and thought he might like to pop round for supper. It was on the spur of the moment, really. But there was no reply.'

'What time was that?'

'About four, I think.'

'The police might be interested to hear that.'

There was a silence, while Una merely sat and Barbara tried to think what to say. She desperately needed to be alone, to give way to the grief which of necessity she had so far suppressed, and which was now welling up inside her; but she owed it to Malcolm's widow to be as calm as she was. To her untold relief, Una stood up.

'I think, if you don't mind, I'd like to go upstairs now.'

'Of course. I'll show you the way. There's a hot-water bottle in the bed and clean towels on the rail.' She lifted the suitcase. 'You have your own toilet things?'

'Yes, thank you.'

The stilted conversation could have been between strangers meeting for the first time, but the formality was helping both of them, as they instinctively realized. Slowly, dragging herself by the banisters like an old woman, Una followed her hostess up the narrow staircase.

There was little more they could do that night. An incident van had arrived, manned by an office manager and skeletal staff. The SOCOs had finished and departed, as had the Coroner's Officer and the pathologist. Finally, the cause of all the activity was wrapped in a body bag and carried out of his home to the waiting hearse. In spontaneous tribute, the officers still at the house silently lined the path as the sombre little procession passed. Then the police guard took up their positions, and the rest of them were free to go.

It was after three when Webb reached his flat, and as he went inside, he noticed a slip of paper which had been pushed under the door. Wearily he stooped to retrieve it. It read: *Come down, whatever time you get home. The front door isn't locked. Hannah.*

Cold, miserable and indescribably weary, he blessed her for her understanding and lost no time in complying. As she'd said, her front door was on the latch and he opened it softly, releasing the catch as he closed it behind him.

A dim light was burning in the hallway, sufficient for him to make his way to her bedroom. The room was silent except for her rhythmic breathing. He undressed quickly, shivering, and slipped into the bed beside her.

'David?'

'Sorry to wake you, but – '

'I wanted you to.' She reached for him. 'My goodness, you *are* cold!'

'And you're gorgeously warm.' He held her closely, his face in her soft hair.

'Was it awful?'

'Pretty bloody. In more ways than one.'

She shuddered, her hands rhythmically rubbing his cold back. 'How was his wife?'

'Remote as always. Impossible to know what she's feeling.'

'Do you want to talk about it?'

'Not at the moment, no.' As the warmth of her body dispelled his coldness, he began to relax for the first time since he'd left her, four long hours before. His eyelids closed as the worst of the horror drained away and, eventually, he slept.

Webb called in at Carrington Street the next morning. There were more people about than was normal for a Sunday, but the atmosphere was subdued, everyone going about their business with none of the usual quips. There was, however, a noticeable feeling of companionship, a drawing together in their shared grief.

Not many of them had known Malcolm personally, Webb realized, but in death he was one of them, an upholder to the best of his ability of law and order, who had been brutally struck down. One and all, they were determined to avenge him.

Alan Crombie looked up from his desk as Webb reached his office. 'Terrible news, Dave.'

'Yep.' Webb paused. 'You live in Coombes Crescent, don't you, Alan? Happen to know a Miss Wood, at number thirty-three?'

'Wood? Can't say I do; we're down at the East Parade end. Why?'

'She's Malcolm's sister-in-law. I must have met her at his wedding, but I don't remember. Anyway, she's looking after his wife for the moment.'

'Anything to go on yet?'

'Precious little. Ray Turner reckons the window was broken *after* the killing, otherwise Malcolm would have heard it and

69

gone to investigate. As it was, he was still sitting in his chair.'

'So what does that mean? That he admitted his killer?'

'Don't know. You'd think if he'd had anyone with him, he'd have turned off the TV. Unless, of course, he'd invited someone to come and watch the match. That might be worth investigating. Anyway, at the moment it *looks* like a break-in, and a malicious one at that. Ornaments deliberately smashed and various things missing, including his ring, which must have been wrenched off his finger after death.'

'Sick,' Crombie commented.

Webb sat down at his desk, dialled the Lethbridge station and spoke for some time, first to the DI, then DS Carter, asking questions, making notes, issuing orders. The house-to-house was already underway.

'I'll be in by four o'clock, in time for the press conference,' he told Carter. 'First, I want to see as many of the family as I can, starting with the widow. At least it's Sunday, so they should all be at home. Have you come up with an address for the younger daughter?'

'No, sir, no one seems to know where she is.'

'I don't want her hearing the news from the media. Pull out the stops, will you, Sergeant? And if you come up with anything, you can reach me on my mobile. See you later.'

He put down the phone and sat staring at it for several minutes, turning possibilities over in his mind. Then, with a sigh, he stood up.

'This is the part I hate,' he commented. 'Still, it's no good putting it off. See you, Alan.'

Jackson was waiting for him, his normally cheerful face sombre. 'Sorry about DCI Bennett, Guv,' he said as they walked out to the car. 'Being a friend of yours, I mean.'

'Thanks, Ken.'

'Do you reckon his death has anything to do with the shop raids?'

'I haven't got round to thinking about that. Seems unlikely; it's not as if he was on to anyone.'

'Someone might have thought he was.'

'Well, it'll be looked into, like all the cases he was working on. Lethbridge have already made a start on it. OK, Coombes Crescent first stop. Number thirty-three.'

Barbara Wood opened the door to them. There were shadows under her eyes, purple as bruises, though she was outwardly calm. Something about her scratched at Webb's memory; he'd seen her somewhere, more recently than either of Malcolm's weddings, but he couldn't think where.

He introduced Jackson and she let them through the bright, narrow hall and showed them into the sitting-room, where Una awaited them. Jackson looked at her with interest; he'd heard the odd comment about the second Mrs Bennett.

She was certainly no beauty, he thought, as the governor introduced him and they sat down; tall and thin, with narrow feet and large, capable hands – a lady, he judged, well able to take care of herself. Her hair, in a short bob, was very dark, as were her eyes under strong, straight brows. Jackson remembered DCI Bennett as an amiable bear of a man, and wondered what on earth had possessed him to marry such a gorgon.

Webb, in his role of interviewer, had thankfully reverted to formality.

'I'd like you to tell me, Mrs Bennett, when you last saw your husband alive.'

'Yesterday morning,' she said at once, her voice low and pleasant. 'He left for work after breakfast, as usual.'

'Do you know what his plans were?'

'He intended to come home at lunchtime and watch the match on television.'

'And you?'

'I went to the hairdresser's in Shillingham, then on to Steeple Bayliss, to sing in a concert. I didn't get back till nearly quarter to eleven.'

Gently he took her through her discovery of the body, which was much as Ray Turner had outlined the previous evening. There was nothing new. 'And I believe some things are missing?' he prompted.

'A few pieces of silver have gone from the dining-room, and the drawers were pulled out of the bureau – looking for money, I suppose.'

'And your husband's ring?'

She looked at him blankly.

'His ring,' Webb repeated. 'He wasn't wearing it. I wondered if you might have removed it, for safekeeping?'

She gave a little shudder. 'No.'

'Were you aware of anyone with a grudge against him? Who might have wished him harm?'

She shook her head positively. 'Malcolm was very easygoing; he didn't make enemies.'

Webb let that pass; in his social life, it was probably true, but there were few policemen who didn't attract hostility merely by doing their job. He changed tack. 'Did he mention inviting anyone to watch the match with him?'

'No, though he might have asked someone at the station.' She stopped, seeing the significance in the question, and her voice grew incredulous. 'You think someone he knew might have killed him?'

'It's surprising he didn't hear the glass breaking.'

She moistened her lips, her wide, unfathomable eyes on his face. 'But if there was a lot of noise on television –'

'Perhaps.'

She leaned forward urgently. 'Mr Webb, you can't really think that? That someone he knew called round, talked with him, and then, when he wasn't expecting it – ?'

'We have to consider all possibilities. Have you by any chance remembered Jane's address?'

She shook her head. 'I'm sorry; Malcolm mentioned it, but it's gone right out of my head.'

'Well, could you give Tim and Sally's to Sergeant Jackson here, while I have a quick word with Miss Wood?'

There was only one other door downstairs, and, after a token tap, he pushed it open to find himself in the kitchen. Barbara Wood turned quickly from the sink and Webb checked in the doorway. Had he not known otherwise, he'd have assumed this was the widow; catching her offguard, he'd surprised such a depth of grief in her eyes that he instinctively looked away.

Rapidly she collected herself. 'Can I help you, Chief Inspector?'

'If you could spare me a moment.' He paused. 'Forgive me – am I right in thinking we've met recently?'

She nodded. 'At Ashbourne, during all that cult business.'

'Of course,' he said, but he was aware of a tweak of surprise. 'I'm sorry, I should have recognized you at the time, but out of context –'

'There's no reason why you should; Malcolm's wedding to my sister was a long time ago, and I wasn't able to get to his second. What can I do for you?'

'When was the last time you saw your brother-in-law?'

'At his birthday dinner.' She gave a half-smile. 'The day you had lunch with him.'

'How did he seem to you?'

'Frankly, I was worried about him. I thought he was unhappy.'

Webb nodded slowly, and she said eagerly, 'You noticed it? I've been wondering if I'd imagined it.'

'I thought he seemed down, certainly, but we all have our bad days.' He'd no intention of telling her about his later conversation with Malcolm. In any case, it was irrelevant now.

'Could it have had any bearing on his death?' she persisted.

'Miss Wood, anything could. At this stage we don't even know if his murder was deliberate. It could have been simply an opportunist break-in that went wrong.'

Barbara nodded, then said diffidently, 'Una thought I should tell you I tried to phone him yesterday afternoon. There was no reply.'

'What time would that have been?'

'Four o'clock; I remember looking at my watch and wondering if he'd be home.'

'Thank you; that might be useful.'

Barbara imagined the phone echoing through the house, while Malcolm –

She said quickly, 'Is there anything else?'

'Not at the moment. I won't hold you up any longer.'

They came out of the kitchen together, and as they did so there was a sudden, staccato ring at the doorbell, then the door burst open and a girl came running into the hall. Barbara gave an exclamation and hurried to meet her.

'Jane! Darling, have you – ?'

The girl flung herself into the older woman's arms. 'Say it isn't true!' she sobbed. 'Please, please, say it isn't true!'

Webb stood awkwardly, unable to pass them in the narrow hallway, and after a moment Barbara Wood put the girl gently from her. 'This is Chief Inspector Webb, darling. He's – looking into the matter for us.'

He smiled at her. 'Hello, Jane, we've been trying to find you. How did you hear about your father?'

'I phoned Steve – my boyfriend – I realized I'd left something at his flat. He said Tim had been trying to get hold of me, so I rang him back.'

Barbara put an arm round her and turned her towards the sitting-room, but the girl stopped abruptly in the doorway, pulling back as she caught sight of Una.

'What's she doing here?' she demanded, her voice starting to rise.

'Jane!' Barbara sounded genuinely shocked. 'Una's staying with me for a few days, until the police have finished at the house.'

'Where were you when Daddy was killed?' Jane cried hysterically. 'If you'd been with him, it wouldn't have happened! But you were *never* there, were you? Why did you marry him, if you didn't want to be with him?'

There was a brief, startled silence, and when Barbara spoke, her voice vibrated with strain. 'Una, I'm sorry; she's in shock. Jane, darling, calm down. This isn't helping anyone.'

Over their shoulders, Webb could see Jackson's surprised face and the motionless figure of Una Bennett, standing as if carved out of stone. He cleared his throat.

'We'll be on our way now,' he said. 'I'll be in touch – '

Jane turned to him swiftly. 'Could you give me a lift home? My friend dropped me off – she said I wasn't fit to drive.'

'But darling, you've only just got here!' Barbara protested. 'Why don't you – ?'

'I'm not staying while she's here,' Jane interrupted. She looked at Webb. 'Please?'

74

Webb met Barbara's eye and shrugged helplessly. 'If that's what you want. Sergeant, would you take Miss Bennett out to the car? I shan't be a minute.'

Jackson, only too eager to escape from the scene, took the girl's arm and led her outside. Webb glanced at Una's expressionless face. 'As your sister-in-law says, she's distraught; she doesn't know what she's saying.'

'On the contrary,' Una answered in her low, clear voice, 'she knows exactly what she's saying. The question is, is she right? *Would* Malcolm still be alive, if I'd been there?'

'It's impossible to say. If it was a personal attack, your presence would only have deferred it.'

'And if it wasn't?'

'Una, don't do this to yourself. We can't all live in each other's pockets.'

Hadn't she said something similar to Barbara, the night of the birthday party?

'All the same,' she said, and for the first time her voice trembled, 'I wish I'd spent more time with him.'

Webb nodded and, unable to think of any further words of comfort, left the two women standing there and went out to the car.

6

Jane was in the back of the car. She had dried her eyes and was twisting her handkerchief round her fingers while Ken Jackson, swivelled to face her, was talking in the voice he used to comfort his own children.

Webb got in beside her. 'Drive on a short way, Ken, then stop. We might as well have our talk with Jane here.'

As Jackson complied, Jane said tremulously, 'You were a friend of Dad's, weren't you? And Mum's as well?'

'Yes, I saw a lot of them at one time.'

She blew her nose. 'We thought, when Mum died, that he'd marry Auntie Barbara.'

Webb looked at her in surprise. Then, remembering the grief on Barbara Wood's face, wondered if she, too, had expected this. In which case, her offer of accommodation to her sister-in-law was doubly generous.

He said carefully, 'Don't you get on with your stepmother?'

In the driving mirror he saw Ken's eyebrows shoot up, but damn it, he had to start somewhere.

'*No one* gets on with her.'

'Why's that?'

'She's so prickly and unapproachable.'

'Perhaps because she knows you don't like her? It can't be easy for her, can it?' He glanced at the girl's rebellious face. 'Your father said you spent a few days at home last week.'

'Yes.'

'And overheard a row they were having?'

She flushed. 'I didn't mean to. It was about her being out all the time. She was even late for his birthday party.'

'Which was why you lashed out at her just now?'

76

Her eyes filled with tears. 'He was *lonely*,' she said.

Webb put his large hand over hers. 'I think she realizes that now, and it's going to make it all the harder for her. She'll need your help, and Tim and Sally's, too.'

Her hand moved protestingly under his, but she made no comment.

'Jane, while you were home those few days, did you get the impression your father was worried about anything? To do with work, perhaps?'

'He told me about the shop raids, but he didn't seem *worried*, just annoyed he hadn't managed to catch anyone.'

'There weren't any unexplained phone calls or anything like that?'

She shook her head.

'And you didn't see anyone hanging round the house?'

'No.' She gave a little gulp. 'I wish I could help you, but I can't.'

'Don't worry about it. All right, we'll run you home, then.' He nodded to Jackson to start the car.

The girl caught at his sleeve. 'Are you going to Sally's now?'

'That's the plan, yes.'

'Could you take me there instead? I – want to be with the family today.'

'Of course.' Poor kid, he thought; she'd been looking for comfort from her aunt, but her stepmother's presence had put paid to that. He could only hope that the divided camps within the family would not complicate the investigation into Malcolm's death.

At one time, the village of Chedbury had been separated from Shillingham by several miles of countryside, but years of ribbon development had almost joined the two. Even so, Chedbury still maintained its village atmosphere with cobbled square and clock tower, the newer cottages melding happily with their older thatched neighbours. And Chedbury woods and common lay only just beyond.

As they were entering the village, Webb's mobile phone rang and he half-turned from the girl beside him to answer it.

'Webb.'

'It's DS Carter, sir. Have you seen the son-in-law yet – Neil Crawford?'

'We're on our way now.' Webb pressed the phone closer to his ear, hoping Carter's voice wouldn't reach Jane.

'Glad I caught you, then. Thought you'd like to know he was in here last week, seeing the governor. Paul Frear, one of our DCs, just happened to mention it.'

'How long did he stay?'

'About ten minutes, Paul thought.'

'Has Frear any idea what he wanted?'

'No, but he said the governor looked pretty down in the mouth when he left.'

'Thanks, Sergeant, that might prove useful. I'll be in touch.'

Webb could tell, by the set of Jackson's neck and shoulders, that he was longing to know *what* might prove useful, but there was no way he could enlighten him in front of Jane. He glanced at the girl slumped beside him.

'Like to guide us the last bit of the way?'

She said listlessly, 'It's the end house on the left.'

The gates were open and, rather than park on the main road through the village, Jackson drove inside, drawing up alongside an immaculate Mercedes. Neil Crawford was doing all right, Webb thought, looking from the sleek car to the solid, double-fronted house.

As he stepped on to the gravel, the front door opened and a young woman stood there, pale and red-eyed. Jane ran stumblingly past him and the two clung together for several minutes. Then Sally Crawford raised her head and met Webb's sympathetic eyes.

'Please come in,' she said unsteadily. 'We've been expecting you.'

The house, he realized, stepping inside, wasn't as large as it appeared, being shallow in structure. A baby's pram took up much of the hallway.

Manoeuvring past it, Webb saw a man standing in one of the doorways, and recognized him from the wedding two years ago. Seeing him again, he remembered his initial and illogical dislike; remembered, too, joking to Hannah later that it was probably jealousy, because Crawford was so good-looking.

He introduced himself and Jackson and turned back to Sally. 'You have our deepest sympathy, you know that. We're all stunned by what's happened.'

She nodded. 'Thank you. Neil, will you take them into the sitting-room, while Jane and I make coffee.'

Crawford stood aside, and the detectives walked past him into a fairly large, square room. A pile of Sunday newspapers lay untouched on the floor, and a baby's jacket was draped over the back of the sofa. Awkwardly, the three men sat down. Webb had no intention of starting the interview, with Crawford's wife due back any minute, and it was he himself who opened the conversation by saying abruptly, 'This is a damnable business.'

'Yes,' Webb agreed unhelpfully. He was aware of Jackson's acute attention as his bright gaze passed between his own face and Crawford's.

'Any idea who might have done it?'

'None, I'm afraid.'

'Where's Una?'

'Staying with Miss Wood at the moment.'

'And that's where you found Jane?'

'She arrived while we were there, yes.'

Crawford gave a sardonic smile. 'And lost no time in leaving again. Understandable, in the circumstances. Tim tried to reach her, but it seems she's left her boyfriend. News to us.'

The small talk was blessedly interrupted by the arrival of Sally and Jane, with a tray and coffee pot respectively. Sally glanced uncertainly at Webb. 'Do you want to speak to us separately, or together?'

Webb registered Crawford's quick frown.

'Separately would be best,' he said equably.

She nodded. 'Then we'll leave you to it.' She poured the coffee, handed it round, and, accompanied by her sister, left the room again, closing the door behind her.

Webb said, 'When did you last see your father-in-law, Mr Crawford?'

There was a brief pause, then Neil replied, 'We were over for his birthday dinner.'

'But you saw him after that, didn't you? At the police station?'

He coloured angrily. 'That was a personal matter.'

'Nevertheless, I'd like to hear about it.'

'Is this really necessary?'

'In the circumstances, yes, it is.'

Crawford sighed ostentatiously. 'If you insist, though I can't see that it's any of your business. I'm having a spot of financial trouble and wondered whether he could help out, that's all.'

'And did he?'

The man mouth tightened. 'No.'

'Which annoyed you?'

'Not to the extent of killing him, if that's what you're implying.'

'I'm implying nothing, Mr Crawford. Nevertheless, his death will presumably ease your financial straits.'

'That's a damnable thing to say!'

'Just how serious are they?'

'I can extricate myself, if that's what you mean, but he could have made it a damn sight easier, if he'd had the mind to.'

'Apart from that, did you get on well with him?'

Another pause, then, presumably deciding honesty was the best policy, 'Not particularly.'

'Why was that?'

'No special reason. I'd nothing really against him, we just weren't kindred spirits.'

What had Malcolm said? *I'm not too keen on Sally's husband.*

'And I suppose your last meeting was acrimonious?'

'Yes.' He looked down at his hands. 'I regret that.'

'Do you know of anyone who had a grudge against him?'

Crawford shook his head.

Webb looked at him consideringly. 'I gather, from your remark earlier, that you don't get on with Mrs Bennett, either?'

Crawford relaxed slightly, more comfortable in denigrating the living. 'The woman's an absolute pain.'

'In what way?'

'She came charging in out of the blue and changed everything. Not only the house and furniture but the whole family atmosphere.'

'Did you know the first Mrs Bennett?'

'Only briefly. She was seriously ill when I met Sally, and died before we were married. If she'd lived, it would all have been very different.'

'But apart from her changing things, which was inevitable, you've nothing concrete against the present Mrs Bennett?'

'I suppose not.'

'Would you say their marriage was happy?'

'Who really knows about someone else's marriage? They seemed all right, but she was as different from Carol as it was possible to be.'

Webb said reflectively, 'Where were you, yesterday afternoon?'

The change of direction seemed to throw Crawford. He stiffened, was on the point of making a vociferous protest, then thought better of it and answered sullenly, 'I went to the DIY then on to the garden centre.'

'Was your wife with you?'

'No, she was still feeding the baby when I left.'

'So you went out at what time?'

'Soon after two, I suppose.'

'And got back when?'

'Going on for four. I couldn't get what I wanted at the first place, and had to search around for it.'

'See anyone you knew?'

'No.' He stared challengingly across at Webb, as though daring him to make some assumption.

But Webb merely said, 'Very well, Mr Crawford, that's all for now. Would you ask your wife to come in, please?'

Sally sat down in the chair her husband had vacated and said flatly, 'I still don't believe it's happened.'

'I'm finding it hard myself.' Webb paused. 'Did you know your husband had asked your father for a loan?'

She flushed. 'Yes, but only afterwards.'

81

'You'd have tried to stop him?'

'Of course I would. We can manage if we have to, without going begging to anyone.'

'Have you got a job yourself?'

'I have, but I'm still on maternity leave. It's meant we've had to pull in the strings a bit.'

'So how did the trouble arise?'

'It was a business deal, which Neil misjudged.'

She was obviously not going to say any more, but Webb could read between the lines. It figured, he thought, and he'd no doubt what Malcolm's reactions would have been.

'How did you spend yesterday afternoon, Sally?'

'Washing and cleaning. Then I went into the garden and did some tidying up.'

'Your husband was out, I gather.'

'Yes, we needed new fencing. It blew down in the gales.'

'What time did he go?'

'While I was feeding Jamie. Two-ish.'

'And got back?'

'In time for tea, about four.'

She looked up suddenly, eyes widening. 'Mr Webb, you surely don't think – ?'

She couldn't put it into words, and he answered quietly, 'These are routine questions, Sally, that's all. Did you know your father would be alone that afternoon?'

'I never gave it a thought.'

'But you knew about the concert?'

'They mentioned it the other evening, but I wasn't really listening. I certainly didn't register which day it was.'

'I know this is a delicate question, but do you think your father was happy?'

'Not as happy as he'd hoped to be, when he married again.' Her voice was shaking.

'Why was that?'

'You must know – you've met her. I can't *imagine* why he didn't marry Auntie Barbara.'

'There's no saying he'd have been any happier.'

82

There was a brief silence, then Sally asked, 'How has Una taken this?'

'She's very shocked, as you'd expect. She's staying with your aunt for now.'

'So Jane said. Oh God, this is a nightmare! First Mum, now Dad. And for him to go like *this*!' Her precarious control snapped and, covering her face with her hands, she wept. Webb, with a nod at Jackson, rose to his feet.

'We'll leave you in peace now,' he said softly. 'If you need to speak to me, you know where I am. Don't bother to show us out.' He patted her shoulder and strode from the room, not even noticing Neil Crawford, who had appeared at the kitchen door.

Out in the drive he stopped and drew a deep breath. The distress of Malcolm's children added to his own grief, but he told himself the best thing he could do, both for them and for Malcolm, was to pursue the investigation to the best of his ability and bring the criminal to justice.

Jackson's footsteps were approaching behind him. Without turning, Webb said, 'I could do with a pint, Ken.'

'Right, Guv. The Magpie's just down the road.'

'Indeed it is. And we can have lunch while we're there.'

He got into the car and sat staring out of the window while Jackson drove the few hundred yards to the pub.

I've done it – I've really done it! I have to keep reminding myself, because part of me still thinks it only happened in my head. I've dreamt about killing him so often, it's hard to believe this time it's true. But he's dead all right – it was on the news and in the papers, and everyone's talking about it.

I keep feeling the ring in my pocket, turning it over and over. Because when I can touch it, solid and real, I know everything else is real, too.

The police are everywhere. They pull out all the stops when one of them gets killed, so I must seem the same as usual, say what people expect me to. And it's not easy, because I'm all churned up – excited, wanting to talk about it – though of course I can't – and at the same time, scared of giving myself away.

It'll be all right, as long as I don't panic. That's something else I keep telling myself. There's no way they could know it was me. But it was – I *killed him! Justice has been done!*

Una let herself out of Barbara's back door and walked slowly down to the bottom of the garden. The morning's sunshine had gone, clouds were banking overhead and it was noticeably colder.

In the next-door garden, washing flapped on a line, white sheets and blue jeans which echoed the colours of the crocuses edging the path. All around her, people were pursuing their normal Sunday routine – doing the washing, eating their roasts, cleaning cars. It was only this house which was set apart, wrapped in a shroud of sudden death, where nothing was normal any more.

Even without sunshine, the outdoor brightness made her eyes ache. Malcolm was dead, murdered. The words meant nothing, though she said them to herself over and over. They were too bizarre, too incredible to comprehend.

What had she been doing at the moment it happened? Driving to Steeple Bayliss? Rehearsing? They hadn't told her exactly when he died – perhaps they didn't know for certain; but whenever it was, no presentiment had reached her, no quiver of alarm or apprehension. Perhaps they'd not been close enough for that.

Was it her fault, as Jane had said, for not being with him? Oh God, Malcolm, I'm sorry – sorry for not being the wife you thought I'd be. You deserved better; I wish I'd spent more time with you.

She stood, alone as always, her face lifted to the grey sky, and the first tears slid from under her closed lids. Though whether she wept for Malcolm or herself, she could not have said.

Barbara stood at the kitchen window, staring down the garden at the motionless figure. She knew she should be feeling sorry for Una, but she wasn't. What she did feel was a deep, resentful anger, that she'd not made Malcolm's last years happier. How she'd have welcomed that chance herself. Yet although Una's grief was as nothing to her own, it was the widow who, to the outside world if not the family, was the main object of sympathy.

Furthermore, while Una was with her she must hold her own anguish in check. It seemed to her distraught imagination that Una was watching her, waiting for her to break down and confess her own love for Malcolm. She was determined that would not happen, which meant that the release of tears was denied her.

Wearily she turned from the window and switched on the dishwasher.

When Webb and Jackson left the Magpie, a few desultory flakes of snow were falling, and by the time they reached the Frecklemarsh road they were in a whirling blizzard.

'We've got off lightly so far this winter,' Webb commented. 'At least it's too wet to lie.'

'It's lying at the moment,' Jackson countered, jerking his head at the grass verges which lay white and glistening on either side. 'Will this be our last call of the day?'

'I'll drop you off on the way back, but there's a press conference in Lethbridge at four. We're going to have the full glare of publicity on this one, Ken, as if it's not already bad enough.'

The village of Frecklemarsh, eight miles south-west of Shillingham, was renowned both for its prettiness, which Webb thought contrived, and as the location of the famed Gables restaurant. However, since the address they'd been given for Tim Bennett was on the Shillingham side of the village, they would not today see either feature.

'Piper's Lane,' Webb mused. 'Must be the new development just past the farm. No doubt old man Piper's made a packet, selling off some of his land.'

Peering through the storm of snowflakes, Jackson negotiated a left-hand turn and came upon four detached houses standing back from the road. The Bennetts' was the third along, but as the gates were closed he had to park outside.

Swearing softly, the two men turned up their collars and hurried up the drive to the house. Their ring was answered by a young woman with long brown hair, who regarded them dubiously.

'Mrs Bennett?'

She nodded and Webb, producing his warrant card, introduced himself and Jackson.

'If the children come, I'll say you're friends of Tim's,' she said quickly as she closed the front door. 'We haven't told them about their grandfather.'

'Where are they now?' Webb asked.

'In the playroom, watching a video. With luck, they won't have heard you.'

'And your husband?'

'I'm sorry, he's not here; he's gone over to see Sally and Jane.'

Damn! So Webb wouldn't, as he'd hoped, get all the family interviews over today. Still, he hadn't let them know he was coming.

Mrs Bennett led them into the sitting-room and sat down, clasping her hands nervously. 'We're stunned,' she said. 'We just can't believe it.'

'I'm very sorry,' Webb said mechanically.

'How's poor Una? It must be ghastly for her.'

Webb tried to hide his surprise. This, apart from Miss Wood's hospitality, was the first sign of compassion for the widow that he had come across. He made a conventional response, then added casually, 'There seems to be friction between her and the rest of the family. Do you know the reason for it?'

Jenny Bennett flushed. 'I get on with her quite well, and she's very good to the children.'

'Your sisters-in-law don't seem to.'

'It's different for them, having to accept her in their mother's place.'

'And your husband?'

'I'm afraid he doesn't like her much, either. I don't think she means to antagonize everyone, it's just her manner. She probably can't help it.'

'Well, it's good to hear some words in her defence. Perhaps Malcolm's death will bring you all closer together.' Though there'd been precious little sign of it so far, Webb added privately.

Apart from that unexpected testimonial, Jenny Bennett had nothing new to tell them. She and Tim had spent the previous afternoon in Erlesborough, buying clothes for the children. She had not heard of anyone who might have a grudge against her father-in-law.

Webb took a note of her husband's business number – a dental surgery in Shillingham – and arranged to phone him the following day. To his relief – and Jackson's disappointment – they managed to leave the house before the children emerged from their playroom.

The snow had stopped, and that which had fallen was melting rapidly on the wet road. As promised, Webb dropped Jackson at his gate as he drove through Shillingham, and set out yet again along the road to Lethbridge. It had been a very long day, and he would be heartily glad when it was over.

7

If Carrington Street station had seemed subdued, the atmosphere at Lethbridge was positively funereal. The last time he'd walked into this foyer, Webb remembered, Malcolm had come through the security door and they'd gone for a drink together. If he could put the clock back, was there anything he could have said or done which might have prevented the tragedy? In all conscience, he couldn't think what.

He was shown into the DI's office and Brian Stratton, pale and drawn, rose from his desk and came to take his hand. Webb had met him a couple of times with Malcolm.

'Of all the bloody things to happen,' he said. 'Malcolm, of all people. Everyone's in a state of total shock. The Super's just left, by the way. He was hoping to catch you, but couldn't wait any longer. Sent his apologies.'

They sat down and he briefly went through the day's events. 'Jeff Carter will give you the latest details; he worked closely with Malcolm. Oh, and Dr Stapleton's away for the weekend, so the earliest we could fix the PM is for tomorrow at nine.'

Webb said heavily, 'That's soon enough for me. I always have to steel myself for PMs, but this will be in a class of its own.'

Carter was waiting for him when he emerged from Stratton's office. 'Could I have a word, sir, before we meet the press?'

'Of course.' Webb noted the 'sir'; to the sergeant, Malcolm was still his governor, and that was as it should be. He had not met Carter before, though he'd heard Malcolm speak well of him. Now, he studied the man, liking his pleasant, slightly chubby face and candid brown eyes.

'It's only a small point and there's probably a simple explanation, but I thought it worth mentioning.' He paused, 'You've not had a chance to interview any of us yet, so you won't know I had lunch with DCI Bennett yesterday, in the canteen.'

Webb eyed him caustically. 'He didn't just happen to mention he was expecting a visitor that afternoon?'

Carter smiled wanly. 'No such luck; but he *did* say that he might as well have lunch here, because his wife was going straight to SB after her hairdo.'

'So?' Webb wondered what the man was getting at.

'That's what she told you, sir?'

'As far as I remember, yes.'

'Well, we've just got the house-to-house reports back, and a couple of the neighbours say they saw Mrs Bennett's car at the house around lunchtime.'

'*What?*'

'That's what I thought. She doesn't seem to have been there long, but all the same it's odd, isn't it?'

Webb frowned. 'What time did you eat?'

'Early, because the governor wanted to get back for the pre-match build-up. We'd finished by about one and he left soon after.'

'And would have been home within ten minutes?'

'That's right, sir. He always walked down.'

'So it's possible, from the reports, that they might have seen each other?'

'That's how it struck me.'

'Well, thanks, Jeff.' He caught Carter's quick glance at the use of his first name. 'No need to be formal, since we'll be working together, eh?'

'No, sir.' Carter hesitated. 'It's not my place to say anything, sir, but I'm glad you're in charge of the case. I know you and the governor were friends.'

'Thanks, Jeff, I appreciate that. Between us, we'll nail the bastard.'

'Or die in the attempt,' Carter said grimly.

'Let's hope it doesn't come to that. Now, I'll just give my sergeant a quick call to check Mrs Bennett's statement, then you can show me where the press conference is.'

'Ken? Sorry to bother you again, but is your pocket book handy? Could you read me what Mrs Bennett said about her movements yesterday?'

He waited while Jackson went in search of it, hearing sounds of noisy play in the background. Then Jackson lifted the phone again.

'Here we are, Guv. *I went to the hairdresser's in Shillingham, then on to Steeple Bayliss, to sing in a concert. I didn't get back till nearly quarter to eleven.* Do you want me to go on?'

Webb gazed reflectively at the wall in front of him. 'No thanks, Ken, that's the bit I wanted. I'll explain in the morning.'

Jeff Carter was waiting at a discreet distance. 'You're right, Jeff,' Webb said grimly. 'No mention of a trip home before the concert.'

The man looked uncomfortable. 'There's something else, too, sir. When PC Ryman at Frecklemarsh went along to his son's house to break the news, the first thing Mr Bennett said was, "Did she do it?"'

'That doesn't surprise me,' Webb commented, conscious that things must be put in perspective before they got out of hand. 'The whole family's convinced Mrs Bennett flies the night skies on her broomstick. Now, let's be on our way; mustn't keep the gentlemen – and ladies – of the press waiting.'

The press conference was much as he'd expected, and he braced himself to answer endless questions about Malcolm's death, while the image of the dead man in his chair burned in his memory. He then made the usual appeal for witnesses – anyone seen arriving at the Bennett house that afternoon, or hanging about at other times.

'DCI Bennett was last seen leaving this station soon after one o'clock yesterday,' he ended. 'We'd like anyone who saw him after that time to contact us immediately. It's always possible he met his killer on the way home and invited him into the house.'

Subsequent questions covered every unsolved crime in the area over the last six months, including the shop raids. Did the police think there was any connection with the chief inspector's death? Webb was thankful that these points were fielded by the press liaison officer, since he'd had no dealings with specifically Lethbridge crime.

It was over at last and, both physically and emotionally drained, he was free to go home. It was six o'clock when he reached the flat and, as before, a note from Hannah had been slid under the door.

Dinner, bed and breakfast at bargain rates, he read. *Apply Flat 7.*

He dialled her number. 'Bless you,' he said. 'How did you guess that's just what I need?'

'It didn't take much working out; after what must have been a harrowing day, I thought you might welcome some company.'

'You're a wonder,' he said gratefully. 'OK if I come down in about an hour? I'd like a long, hot bath first.'

'Just don't fall asleep in it!' she warned.

When he arrived at Hannah's flat just after seven, an appetizing smell of roasting meat reached him, reminding him of the time that had elapsed since his ploughman's at the Magpie in Chedbury.

'You look exhausted,' Hannah said. 'Come and sit down while I get you a drink.'

'It's not a day I'd like to live through again,' he admitted, settling himself in the depths of the apple-green chair. He leaned his head back and closed his eyes, then opened them again to banish the crowd of images that jostled against the screen of his lids; images he preferred not to remember.

Hannah handed him his glass. 'You've been visiting the family?'

'Yes, always traumatic in such cases.'

'Especially when you know them.'

'I don't exactly know them; I've seen them from time to time over the years, but only fleetingly. I saw more of them as babies, when Susan and I used to go round to the house.'

He seldom mentioned his ex-wife, and it was proof to Hannah of how deeply this case was affecting him. She realized achingly that a part of his own life, his past, his memories, had also been brutally terminated.

'Did they remember you?' she asked, gently bringing him back to the present.

'They knew who I was, not much more than that.'

'How's the widow bearing up?'

'In the accepted phrase, as well as can be expected. A bit better, in fact. And here's an interesting thing.' He paused to sip his drink. 'She's staying with Carol's sister for the moment, and do you know who she is?'

Hannah shook her head. 'Surprise me.'

'I might, at that. She's one of your lot, at the school.' Hannah was deputy head of the prestigious Ashbourne School for Girls, and for the last six months had been in charge of it while the head was on a sabbatical.

She raised her eyebrows. 'Really? Who?'

'Miss Barbara Wood.'

'Barbara Wood's Malcolm's sister-in-law?'

'That's right.'

'Good Lord!'

'I gather you didn't know.'

'Well, no, but until this weekend it wouldn't have meant anything to me if I had.'

'What's your opinion of her?'

'I like her very much. She's intelligent, conscientious, an excellent teacher –'

'I'm not asking for a reference, Hannah!' Webb interrupted. 'What are your personal impressions?'

'She's always struck me as calm and level-headed, a good person in a crisis.'

'Do you know anything of her private life?'

'Only that she lives alone, travels extensively during school holidays, enjoys the theatre and is knowledgeable about flowers and plants.'

'Love affairs?'

'That's something I don't discuss with my staff,' Hannah answered primly, her eyes mocking him.

'But have you heard any man's name in connection with her?'

'Look, what is this? You haven't lined her up as murderer, I trust?'

'No,' Webb said slowly, 'but I'm pretty damn sure she was in love with Malcolm.'

'Her sister's husband?'

'It does happen,' Webb returned drily.

'I know it happens, damn it, but – Barbara?'

'I caught her offguard in the kitchen, and the expression on her face –' He broke off, shrugging. 'What's more, all the kids expected him to marry her when Carol died.'

'They knew she loved him?'

'Oh, I don't think so, just thought it would tie up loose ends. And God knows, the poor bloke would have been better off with her than with Una.'

'You don't like Una any better, then?'

'To be honest, I don't know what I think of her. Occasionally there's a vulnerable look in her eyes, but just as I start to feel sorry for her, she comes out with something caustic and I change my mind again. The daughter-in-law was the only one with a good word to say for her.'

'And Barbara? She offered her hospitality, at least.'

'Barbara,' Webb said, 'is doing her duty, as she sees it. I don't think she's enjoying it much.'

He stared into his glass, wondering why Una hadn't told him she'd been back to the house. He'd ask her tomorrow, but it was not something he could discuss with Hannah. Not yet, anyway.

In the little house in Coombes Crescent the evening was coming to an end, to Barbara's intense relief. Conversation was increasingly stilted and Una spent much of the time gazing silently into space. Barbara would have given a lot to know what she was thinking.

'I'll ring school in the morning,' she said, breaking a lengthening silence. 'I'm sure they'll give me a day or two off, in the circumstances. It's compassionate leave, after all.'

Una turned to her in surprise. 'Don't you feel up to going in?'

'It's not that,' Barbara denied – too quickly, she felt. 'But I can hardly leave you here alone, and –'

'Oh, I shan't be here, Barbara. I'm going to the office in the morning.'

Barbara gazed at her, astounded. 'You're going in to work *tomorrow*? Less than forty-eight hours after Malcolm died?'

'What's that got to do with anything?' Una demanded, with a touch of her old impatience. 'My hanging around here isn't going to help him, is it, and I've several important appointments. Anyway, work will help to take my mind off things. I should have thought you'd feel the same.'

Barbara was at a loss how to reply. Though she'd dreaded another day of Una's exclusive company, it had, to her mind, been part of the package deal she'd offered her. Her own control, reined in of necessity, was increasingly unstable and she certainly didn't feel ready to resume normal life as if nothing had happened. But if Una went to work, she herself could hardly stay at home.

'Just as you like,' she said weakly at last, and that was how the matter rested. As she prepared for bed and another sleepless night, Barbara, holding back tears until her throat ached, told herself bitterly that at least Una's long silences were now explained: she'd been planning the next day's appointments.

Webb and Hannah lay side by side in her bed. She had thought he might be too tired for lovemaking, but she was wrong. He'd seemed to need her more than ever, perhaps as reassurance that, despite his friend's death, he himself was still alive.

It was in this aftermath that, often, confidences came. If a case was troubling him he'd use her as a sounding board, bouncing off ideas which were too unformed to put to more official recipients. Or he'd speak of the horrors he'd witnessed, of dead children, mutilated bodies, distraught relatives. Hannah dreaded these confidences, and it took all her strength not to beg him to stop, but she somehow managed to keep silent, knowing it was a release for him, and one which he could obtain nowhere else.

Tonight, therefore, she was not surprised when he started speaking of Malcolm Bennett. At first his tone was nostalgic, recalling their first meeting, evenings spent together with their wives. He told her of Bennett's passion for football, the matches they'd been to, the celebrations and disappointments.

Then the reminiscing became more sombre. It had been to David that Malcolm first confided the news of Carol's illness, and to whom he had turned for comfort during the dark months that followed; David, also, who'd been the first to hear of his plans to remarry.

'I wanted to like her, Hannah, for Malc's sake, but I couldn't. I hope he never knew that.'

'I'm sure he didn't,' she murmured.

'I'm just beginning to realize how much I'll miss him,' he said. 'God, if I could only –' He came to a halt, his hand tightening convulsively on hers.

'I know, darling, I know.' She put her arms round him and held him till the tension gradually left him and he slid into sleep.

Carefully, so as not to disturb him, Hannah lay back on her pillows, hoping that the day ahead would deal more kindly with him; hoping, too, that she'd been some comfort. And she thought of Barbara Wood, who, if David was right, was bearing a grief deeper than her family appreciated.

Resolving to keep a tactful eye on her, Hannah in her turn fell asleep.

The postmortem the next morning was as grim as Webb had feared, but no new facts emerged. In layman's terms, Malcolm had died from three heavy blows to the skull administered from above and behind, which they had known all along. The discarded stick was officially confirmed as the murder weapon – the traditional 'blunt instrument' – and the time of death, based on the stomach contents, estimated at between one-thirty and two.

White-faced, Webb thankfully emerged from the hospital

and drove down to the police station to meet Jackson as arranged and inform him of the discrepancy in Mrs Bennett's statement.

Jackson, noting but not commenting on his boss's pallor, remarked, 'So there's another possibility: they both got back around the same time, had another row like the one the girl came in on, and she lost her temper and thumped him.'

'Theoretically it's possible, though she's unlikely to have had that stick to hand.'

'Why else would she pretend she didn't go back?'

'Don't ask me, Ken. Once we've seen the neighbours and heard what they have to say, we'll pay her another visit. I'd like to track down Jane's boyfriend, too. It's a long shot, but he might have been harbouring some kind of resentment.'

The addresses Carter had given Webb were of two houses on the opposite side of the road from the Bennetts, one directly facing them, the other a little way down. The incident van was still parked outside, but this was a quiet neighbourhood with little passing traffic, and Webb didn't see anyone approach it.

He and Jackson went up the path of number twenty-six. The door was opened by an elderly man in a hand-knitted cardigan, who cupped a hand to his ear before Webb so much as opened his mouth. He hoped devoutly there would be someone else to speak to, and he was in luck. Halfway through Webb's explanation of his presence, the man turned and shouted back into the house, 'Mother! It's the police!'

An equally elderly woman came hurrying up the hall, but she was spry and sharp-featured and showed no sign of her husband's deafness.

'About Mr Bennett, is it? Crying shame, I call it, a nice man like that, murdered in his own bed.'

'His own chair, anyway,' Webb amended smilingly, complying with her gesture to step inside. 'You know the family well, ma'am?'

The woman's mouth pursed. 'I knew the first Mrs Bennett. Lovely woman, she was – never minded lending a hand. She made jam every year for the WI and collected regular for charity.' She sniffed. 'But this one's too hoity to talk to the likes of us.'

Someone else Una had offended. Webb had an irrational desire to shake her; *why* did she have to antagonize everyone?

'I believe you saw her car on Saturday?'

'That's right. I was pulling up weeds at the front. Just decided to stop and see to lunch, when she came up the road and turned into her drive. Don't know why everyone's so interested; she lived there, after all.'

'Could you say what time this was, Mrs – er – Hill?'

'Well, like I said, I was thinking about lunch. Must have been getting on for one.'

'You can't be more specific?'

'We eat when we feel like it,' she said, fixing him with a beady eye. 'We don't have gongs going off at set times.'

Webb let that go. 'How long was she there?'

She shrugged. 'It was two before I got outside again, and the car'd gone by then. She could have put it in the garage, I suppose, but I've never known her to. Mr Bennett keeps his in there, and she always leaves hers in the drive.'

'Did Mr Bennett come home while you were in the garden?'

'If he did, I didn't see him. Hardly surprising, since I was on my knees most of the time, pulling up weeds. I only saw her because I happened to stand up just as she arrived.'

'And you didn't see anyone else call at the house?'

She shook her head firmly.

'Might your husband – ?' Webb asked tentatively, eyeing the old man who was looking from face to face as they spoke, apparently catching little of what was said.

'Him!' said his wife scornfully. 'Spends most of his time asleep in his chair.'

'So you would say Mrs Bennett arrived home about one and had gone again by two?'

She nodded and Webb could do little but thank her and take his leave. All she'd told them was that she'd seen Una around lunchtime, which they'd been aware of when they arrived. They were no nearer knowing how closely her return coincided with her husband's.

It was with reduced expectations that they walked along the pavement to the second address.

Mrs Higham at number eighteen was very different from her neighbour, a smart, well-dressed woman in her forties. She ushered them into her sitting-room, produced coffee in china cups and settled them comfortably on the sofa – a distinct improvement, Jackson felt, on the conversation they had just held in the hall up the road.

But she began with the same point as Mrs Hill. 'I don't know what's so unusual in my having seen Mrs Bennett,' she said, surveying them with thinly disguised curiosity. 'When the police asked if I'd seen anyone going into their house, I said no. It was only when they persisted, "Anyone at all?", that I mentioned her.'

Webb sidestepped the implied question. 'And how did you come to see her, ma'am?'

'I'd been shopping in town, and as I reached the roundabout at the bottom of the hill, she was approaching along the Shillingham road. I had right of way and she waited for me, though I don't think she recognized me. She followed me up the hill and into Westwood Avenue, where, of course, I turned into my gateway and she went on to hers.'

'And what time would that have been?'

'A quarter to one,' she answered promptly.

A definite time at last! 'Can you be sure of that?'

'Absolutely. I was listening to *The News Quiz* on Radio 4, and as I stopped the car I glanced at the clock to see how much longer the programme had to run and saw there were ten minutes – it finishes at five to one. So I hurried inside and turned on the radio in the kitchen.'

'Thank you, Mrs Higham, that's very helpful,' Webb said, for once meaning it.

She raised her eyebrows. 'Is it? I can't think why?'

Again he avoided her question with one of his own. 'Did you happen to notice what time Mrs Bennett *left* the house?'

'In the morning, you mean?'

'No, after she'd returned home.'

'I didn't even know she had. Oh.' She stopped, seeming suddenly to realize the implications. 'Of course, she must have done, or her poor husband would never have been killed.'

That, Jackson told himself, scribbling in his pocket book, was a moot point.

Webb was silent, mentally summarizing the situation. They now knew for a fact that Una had arrived home at twelve-forty-five, but still had no idea how long she'd stayed. Nor had they a definite time for Malcolm's return; no one seemed to have seen *him*. He might, as Carter supposed, have gone straight home – and in view of the imminent football match, that was the most likely theory. But he could have stopped off somewhere first, perhaps for a sports paper or some cans of beer to drink during the match.

Without corroborating evidence, though, it must be assumed that he arrived home at about one-fifteen – half an hour after Una. Why had she gone back to the house? To see him? And even if so, would she have waited so long when, as Malcolm had told him, she had a rehearsal that afternoon in Steeple Bayliss? For that matter, what could have been so urgent that she would go out of her way like that, when she'd seen her husband at breakfast and expected to see him again that evening? Whatever it was, wouldn't a phone call have sufficed?

Webb looked up from his ponderings to find Mrs Higham's bright eyes considering him.

She said hesitantly, 'Although I didn't see anyone near the house on Saturday, there *was* a young man hanging about earlier.'

Webb snapped back to attention. 'When was that?'

'About ten days ago. He was parked outside the Bennetts' one evening. I noticed him when I was taking my daughter to ballet – it's only round the corner, so we walk – and he was still there when I came back ten minutes later. I was slightly concerned, and looked out of the window a couple of times.'

'To check on him?'

'Yes; he was there for a while, but the last time I looked, he'd gone.'

'What day would that have been?'

'Wednesday; that's when Sophie has her class.'

'Last Wednesday?'

'No, the week before.'

'And you haven't seen him since?'

'No.'

'You didn't think of telling the Bennetts someone was watching their house?'

She moved uncomfortably. 'I'd no reason to think he was, particularly. I mean, yes, he was parked outside, but he might have been waiting for someone. Anyway, with Mr Bennett being in the police, I thought he probably knew about it.'

'It doesn't make us psychic,' Webb said mildly. 'Did you get a good look at him?'

'No, we were on the other side of the road. All I registered was that he was young and wearing some kind of dark jacket. He had the car radio on – we could hear it.'

'And the car itself?'

'Oh yes – I've just remembered! As I passed it coming home I memorized the number, just in case.'

Webb's face lit up. 'Wonderful! That could be very useful. You have still got it?' he added with sudden anxiety.

'Only because I'd forgotten all about it.' She stood up, took a piece of paper from behind the clock, and handed it to him.

'That's great; thank you very much, Mrs Higham. I wish everyone took their civic duties so seriously.' And he closed his mind to the possibility that, had she reported the matter at the time, Malcolm might still be alive. But that was wild theorizing and had no basis in fact. As she'd said, the young man could have been innocently waiting for his girlfriend.

When they left her shortly afterwards, Webb and Jackson called at the incident van, handed over the car registration and, while they waited for it to be checked, told the men about the two interviews.

'How's SOCO getting on at the house?' Webb asked the manager.

'Not much new, Guv. A few hairs, some fibres and a smudged footprint in the kitchen, but not clear enough to be useful. He wore gloves, of course.'

'Anyone been in to see you?'

'Not after the first novelty wore off. I reckon we'll be moving back to the station soon.'

Webb nodded, then turned as the answer came back on the car. It was a blue Ford Escort, registered in the name of Steven John Clark.

'Steve Clark?' Jackson broke in excitedly. 'Guv, that's young Jane's boyfriend. I got his name and address from Mrs Bennett.'

'Is it, by Jove? Come to think of it, Ken, it fits. That Wednesday would have been while Jane was staying at the house. He was probably just hoping for a word with her, but it'll do no harm to check. Any idea where he works?'

'At Savemore's in Duke Street.'

'Then we'll head back to Shillingham, call on him and then Mrs Bennett and see what they both have to say for themselves. Thanks, lads. I'll be in touch later.'

Webb went quickly down the steps, Jackson at his heels, and they got into the car. As the sergeant started it and they moved away, Webb reflected that the next couple of hours should prove interesting. With luck, they might also prove instructive.

8

It was eleven-thirty by the time they got back to Shillingham, and the supermarket car park was crowded. Dodging between trolleys, Webb and Jackson made their way inside and asked a girl on the checkout where Steven Clark was.

'Stacking the shelves in aisle four, last time I saw him,' she replied without looking up.

He was still there. Rounding the corner into the aisle, Webb took advantage of a minute or two's undetected inspection of their quarry. He was a tall young man, with the kind of brash good looks that would appeal to an impressionable girl, though his hair was overlong for Webb's taste. He was engaged in lifting giant packs of cereals from the box at his feet and arranging them on the shelves above, without – and here Webb didn't blame him – any open show of enthusiasm for the task. He wore a blue uniform overall with a badge on his lapel that confirmed his identity. To Webb, he looked depressingly like dozens of other young men he'd faced in interview rooms over the years. He wouldn't trust him as far as he could throw him, but that didn't make him a murderer.

He moved slowly down the aisle, past young mothers with fractious children and elderly ladies peering at illegible shopping lists.

'Mr Clark?' he said pleasantly.

The young man turned, and as he caught sight of Webb and the card he was holding, his eyes widened in alarm. Jackson tensed, thinking he was going to make a run for it. Then the moment passed and the governor was adding, 'We'd like a word.'

Clark's eyes darted about as beads of sweat broke out on his forehead. 'What about? I haven't done anything.'

'Is there somewhere we could talk?'

He shook his head, looking nervously over his shoulder, but if he was hoping to delay the interview, he was out of luck. 'Then we'll go to the car park,' Webb said.

Clark made one last, desperate attempt at evasion. 'But I'm not supposed –'

'I'll explain, if the need arises.'

In silence the three of them went out of the automatic doors and down the steps. Webb made for the area with the fewest cars, and turned to face the young man. Jackson, propping himself against a handy Vauxhall, took out his pen and pocket book.

'Now, you are Steven John Clark of fifty-nine, Dick Lane, Shillingham?'

A nod.

'And you own a blue Ford Escort, registration number H 674 DGH?'

Clark looked bewildered. 'Is it the tax disc? I thought –'

'Are you the owner of that car?'

'Yeah.' He waited nervously, his fingers twisting at the buttons on his overall.

'Could you tell me, sir, why you were parked outside twenty-three, Westwood Avenue, Lethbridge on the evening of Wednesday the eighth of March?'

'Twenty – ?'

'The home,' Webb said inexorably, 'of DCI Bennett, who was murdered last Saturday.'

Bewilderment turned swiftly to panic. 'Oh, now look, you can't pin that on me! I'd never –'

'No one,' Webb said clearly, 'is trying to pin anything on anyone. You don't deny you were outside the house that evening?'

'I dunno what date it was, but his daughter's my girlfriend. She'd gone back home and I wanted to speak to her.'

'And did you?'

'No; I was going to go and knock, but decided not to.'

'You took your time deciding.'

'No law against that, is there?'

'How long have you known Miss Bennett?'

He shrugged. 'Two, three years.'

'You were both living at the same address, I believe?'

'Yeah.'

'But not any longer?'

Clark flushed and shook his head.

'What about last Saturday? Did you go back to the house again, looking for her?'

'No!' The reply was instant and emphatic.

'What *did* you do last Saturday, Mr Clark?'

'I was working, wasn't I?'

'All day?'

His eyes fell. 'Most of it.'

'What time did you leave here?'

There was a pause, then he said unwillingly, 'All right, if you must know I skived off early. Three-ish, I suppose.'

Damn! Webb thought. It would be checked, of course, but allowing for the estimated time of death and the fact that Lethbridge was a twenty-minute drive away, he was probably in the clear. Nevertheless, something was evidently bothering the lad and he smoothly continued with his questioning.

'Where did you go?'

'Home, to watch the match.'

'Any of your friends with you?'

He shook his head.

'So after about three o'clock, no one can confirm where you were?'

'I told you, I was at home.' Clark's voice had risen, and a woman loading her shopping into the boot of her car turned and stared at them.

Webb tried another angle. 'You'd met Mr Bennett, I suppose?'

'Once or twice,' Clark answered sullenly. 'I should have gone to his birthday dinner, but I copped out.'

'Why was that?'

'Me and Jane were having problems, and the last thing I needed was an evening with her bloody family.'

'So when was the last time you saw him?'

'Around Christmas, I suppose.'

'Did you get on well?' Webb asked, knowing the answer.

The young man snorted. 'What do you think? Didn't like us living together, did he?'

'And you resented his influence on Jane?'

Clark's eyes fell and he did not reply.

'When she went home for those few days,' Webb persisted, 'were you worried he might persuade her not to go back to you?'

''Course I was. That's why I went there.'

'But she did come back.'

'Only for about a week, then she left for good.'

'And you blamed her father?'

'And that aunt of hers, the schoolteacher. She didn't like me, I could tell.' He said suddenly, 'Has Jane said anything?'

'About what?'

He coloured and looked away. 'Doesn't matter.'

Webb regarded him thoughtfully. Another word with Jane could be beneficial.

'You've nothing else to tell us, Mr Clark?'

He shook his head.

'Very well; that's all for the moment.'

Clark glanced from Webb to Jackson and back again, an expression of almost ludicrous relief on his face. 'You mean I can go?'

'For the moment, yes.'

He needed no second telling, but started off towards the doors of the supermarket at a loping run. The two detectives stood looking after him.

'He's hiding something, Guv,' Jackson opined.

'I'm with you on that, Ken. Jane might know what.'

'No saying if she'd tell us, though.'

'We'll face that when the time comes, but for the moment, Mrs Bennett is our next port of call.'

But the house in Coombes Crescent seemed to be deserted. Webb rang and knocked several times before a woman coming up the path next door volunteered the information that Miss Wood was out.

'Out where, ma'am, do you know?'

'At school, I should think. She teaches at Ashbourne, you know.' It was said with respect, and Webb hid a grin.

'What about the lady who's staying with her?' he asked.

'Oh, I don't know anything about that.'

Webb nodded his thanks and the woman let herself into the adjoining house.

'She wouldn't have gone to work and left Mrs Bennett alone, Ken,' he said. 'Which leaves us with only one conclusion: *she* must have gone back to work, too.'

Jackson was scandalized. 'Two days after her husband was murdered?'

'It's known as the stiff upper lip,' Webb said. 'Or something,' he added darkly, walking back down the path. 'Did you get her work address?'

'Yes, Guv.' Jackson fumbled through the pages of his pocket book. 'Drew's Translation Services, Lowther Building, King Street.'

'Off we go, then.'

King Street was, as usual, congested with traffic and Jackson pulled up on a yellow line while Webb scribbled 'Police on official duty' and propped the note and log book on the dashboard.

According to the ornate board in the foyer, the firm they wanted was on the second floor, and as they emerged from the lift they were confronted by a frosted glass door bearing its name. Webb pushed it open and they went inside.

The foyer in which they found themselves would have done credit to a country house – thick carpet, flowers, sofas, and low tables stacked with magazines. An attractive woman at a mahogany desk looked up and smiled at them.

'Good morning, gentlemen. Have you an appointment?'

Webb introduced himself and Jackson, seeing her expression change. 'Is Mrs Bennett in?'

'Er – yes, yes, she is. Just one moment and I'll tell her you're here.'

She did not, as Webb expected, lift the intercom on her desk, but went along a short passage, knocked at a door, and disappeared inside. A peaceful silence descended, though he was aware that behind the closed doors a number of people were hard at work. Only ten years ago, the air would have been filled with the clatter of typewriters. Now, word-processors made life more pleasant not only for their operators but for everyone in the vicinity.

The receptionist reappeared and beckoned to them and they obediently walked towards her, their feet silent on the thick carpet.

Una Bennett was seated at her desk and rose as they entered the room. She was wearing the same navy suit as the last time they'd seen her, and Webb reflected that she had not yet been allowed home to replenish her wardrobe.

'Good morning, Mrs Bennett. You've taken some tracking down; we went to Coombes Crescent looking for you.'

Her hand was cool in his. 'There was nothing useful I could do there,' she said. 'How can I help you, Chief Inspector? Has there been a development? Please sit down, both of you.'

She gestured towards two chairs facing her desk and sat down again behind it. Webb was ironically aware of the change in status thus established.

'There seems to be an inconsistency in your statement,' he began. 'We understood, from what you told us, that you went to the hairdresser's in Shillingham, then on to the rehearsal in Steeple Bayliss?'

'Yes?'

'That's correct?'

'Of course.'

'Then can you explain how two of your neighbours report having seen you at home around one o'clock?'

She stared at him for a moment, then her face cleared. 'How stupid of me – I quite forgot. While I was at the hairdresser's, I realized I'd left my blouse at home, and I needed it for the concert. I had to make a detour to collect it.'

'How long were you at the house?'

'Less than two minutes. I ran straight upstairs, took it out of the airing-cupboard, and left again at once. As it was, I was almost late for rehearsal.'

As simple as that, Webb thought. It had the ring of truth about it. But still –

'You didn't see your husband while you were there?'

'Of course not. He wasn't in.'

'He must have arrived soon afterwards.'

'So?' She regarded him coolly. 'Are you suggesting I lay in wait for him and killed him before going on to the concert?'

To his annoyance, Webb felt at a disadvantage. 'Of course not, but we like to tie up loose ends.'

'It's a pity my neighbours have nothing better to do than report my comings and goings.' Her eyes narrowed. 'Or did you send someone to ask specifically if they'd seen me?'

'House-to-house inquiries were made as a matter of course,' Webb answered stiffly, 'and everyone was asked who they'd seen entering or leaving the house.'

'Talk about the net-curtain brigade,' she said scornfully.

'Not appropriate, actually, Mrs Bennett,' Webb was stung to retort. 'One lady was working in her garden, and you followed the other home up the hill. Perhaps you didn't notice her.'

She was frowning slightly, turning her pen in her fingers. 'Did they report seeing anyone else?'

'No, why?'

'I've just remembered an odd sensation I had as I was leaving the house. As though I wasn't alone.'

'You heard a noise of some sort?'

'No, of course not,' she exclaimed impatiently, 'or I'd obviously have investigated. It was – just a feeling, something I can't explain. I decided I was imagining it.'

'But now you're not so sure? Did you go in the kitchen?'

'I glanced into both it and the sitting-room, wondering if Malcolm was home after all – in fact, I think I called his name – but no one was there.'

'And obviously there was no glass on the kitchen floor?'

'Obviously not.'

Webb studied her, trying to see what attraction she'd held for Malcolm. Her skin was excellent, he conceded, her nose straight and her eyes, as he'd told Hannah, striking. Yet she would never be described as pretty. And suddenly he realized what she lacked: that innate ability to make the most of her assets, present herself to advantage. Instead, she'd developed a brusque, take-it-or-leave-it attitude which had the effect of making his – and seemingly many other people's – hackles rise.

He thought sardonically of those old American films where the plain but efficient heroine suddenly removes her spectacles, to become instantly and unexpectedly beautiful. But Una had no spectacles to remove.

She looked up, catching his eyes on her, and he said quickly, 'Can you think of anything unusual that happened in the last few weeks, either at home or to do with Malcolm's work?'

'No, nothing.'

'Jane's visit the other week?' Webb prompted.

Una stared at him. 'What on earth – ?'

'It doesn't have to be something significant, Mrs Bennett, just anything at all that was out of the ordinary, someone visiting who'd not been before, for instance?'

'Well, as you say, Jane was with us for a couple of nights, but there's been nothing else that I can think of.'

'No one came to the house for the first time?' Webb persisted.

'Only the new cleaner.'

'When did she start?'

'The day after Malcolm's birthday – the seventh. She comes twice a week – which reminds me, she's due again tomorrow.' Her voice ended interrogatively.

'I doubt if Scenes of Crime will have finished by then. Could I have her name and address?'

'Mrs Jones, but I've no idea where she lives. I suppose I have a note of it somewhere.'

'Do you employ anyone else – a gardener, for instance?'

'No, my husband does – did the garden himself.'

'What about tradesmen – laundry, newspaper deliveries, postmen? Any of them change lately?'

'If they had, I wouldn't have known. The only one I see is the postman, and then only if something won't go through the box. The laundry comes on Fridays while the cleaner's there – I leave money ready – and the newspapers are paid monthly by cheque.' Her impatience began to show through again. 'Though how any of those people can have the remotest connection with Malcolm's death, I can't imagine.'

Nor could Webb. Signalling to Jackson, he got to his feet, thanked Una for her help, and left her to return to her work.

It was during the lunch break that Hannah, coming out of her study, almost collided with Barbara Wood.

The woman murmured an apology and would have hurried on, but Hannah, alarmed by her pallor, caught at her arm.

'Miss Wood, can you spare me a moment?'

She gave a quick, desperate little smile. 'If you don't mind, Miss James, not just – '

A group of girls came chattering down the corridor, drowning her words. They broke off on seeing the members of staff, and continued to the dining hall in the obligatory silence. As they passed, Barbara instinctively turned her face away from them and Hannah was shocked by the strain on it. She drew her into the study and closed the door.

'Sit down, Barbara. You look in need of a breathing space.' The two women had become friends over the years, and used each other's Christian names when they were alone.

Barbara remained standing, looking towards the door as if undecided whether to stay. Then she gave a choking little gasp and her face crumpled. Covering it with her hands, she began to weep, deep, shuddering sobs racking her body.

Hannah put an arm round her and guided her to a chair. Then, walking to the window, she stood looking out at the gravel drive and the high nets bordering the tennis courts until the painful sobbing behind her had eased.

'I'm so sorry,' Barbara said at last in a clogged voice. 'I've been fighting this all morning, and was making for the privacy of the cloakroom – '

' – when I waylaid you? I could see something was very wrong.' Hannah came back and perched on the edge of her desk. Though she knew the reason for Barbara's distress, she could not refer to it unless Barbara herself confided in her.

Which, to Hannah's relief, she proceeded to do. 'We've had a family bereavement,' she explained. 'That police inspector who was murdered at the weekend was my late sister's husband.'

'Oh Barbara, I'm so sorry. How ghastly for you.'

'I have his – widow staying with me at the moment, and felt I owed it to her not to break down. But of course it's brought back my sister's death, and it suddenly all got too much.'

'Isn't it rather soon to be back at work?'

'Yes,' Barbara admitted, 'but since Una – his widow – was determined to go in today, I could hardly do otherwise.'

Hannah looked pityingly at the white face and swollen, reddened eyes. David suspected Barbara might have been in love with Malcolm, but she'd explained the intensity of her grief by referring back to her sister's death, which was quite plausible.

She said – since she wasn't supposed to know – 'Are there any children?'

Barbara nodded and blew her nose. 'Grown up, of course, two of them married. But they've lost both parents in little over two years, and both of them well before their time.'

'And his second wife – do they all get on well?' Hannah felt justified in her probing; on the one hand, she sensed Barbara wanted – needed – to talk, and she herself seemed to be the only one to whom she could speak freely. And secondly, there was the possibility she might learn something useful to David.

'Unfortunately not,' Barbara was replying, her voice a little stronger now, which seemed to confirm Hannah's diagnosis. 'She can be difficult and the family find her heavy going, I'm afraid.'

'How has she taken her husband's death?'

'Better than I have,' Barbara retorted, then bit her lip.

Hannah felt it wise to call a break. 'Look, you must eat to keep up your strength, but you're in no fit state to go into the dining hall. Shall we have lunch on a tray in here? It would give you a chance to relax and rally your forces for the afternoon classes. Unless, of course, you'd rather go home? I'd quite understand if you would.'

Barbara looked up at her gratefully. 'That's awfully kind of you, Hannah; I'll be all right for the afternoon, but lunch in here would be perfect. Thank you for being so understanding.'

'Fine, then while I organize it I suggest you go and wash

your face. It will make you feel better.' And, with a little nod of approval as Barbara obediently rose to her feet, Hannah lifted the intercom.

Fortified by lunch at the Brown Bear, Webb and Jackson set off to interview the last member of the Bennett family, Tim, at the dental surgery in Kimberley Road.

'The smell's enough to give me the heebie-jeebies,' Jackson confided as they pushed open the door, 'let alone the sound of that drill. My teeth are starting to ache in sympathy!'

Webb strode up to the counter, where three receptionists sat behind plaques bearing the names of the three dentists. 'I'd like to see Mr Bennett,' he told the appropriate young woman.

'Have you an appointment, sir?'

'No, I'm Chief Inspector Webb; it's about his father's death.'

Her face sobered. 'Of course, sir. If you'll just wait till he's finished with this patient, I'll slip you in before his next appointment.'

'Thank you.'

Webb glanced into the open-plan waiting-room alongside and, since there was no help for it, perched on one of the less than comfortable chairs, Jackson beside him. Three or four people were dotted about, pretending, through concentrated reading of their magazines, that they hadn't heard the conversation at the counter. Webb wondered which was Tim's next patient; no doubt he or she would be simmering with resentment at the anticipated delay.

A door opposite opened and a woman and child came out. Webb looked up expectantly, but one of the other receptionists called, 'Mr Hayward, please,' and an elderly man near Jackson got hurriedly to his feet and disappeared into the room.

The next door to open seemed more hopeful. As a youth emerged, Tim's receptionist came out from behind the counter and went in, appearing a moment later to call, 'Chief Inspector – if you'd like to come through now?'

Webb lumbered to his feet, glad of release from the constricting chair. Tim Bennett, wearing a white coat, came to meet him with his hand extended.

'Mr Webb – good to see you again, even under these circumstances. Do sit down.'

Webb introduced Jackson, who avoided looking at the dental instruments as he took the indicated seat. Tim Bennett, being the eldest of Malcolm's children, was the one Webb remembered most clearly. He was a thickset young man with rather a heavy face, already, at thirty, showing signs of developing his father's jowls. He had thick, tow-coloured hair, slightly darker than his sisters', and hazel eyes.

'Sorry I missed you at the house,' he was saying. 'Jenny said you'd called.' He rubbed a hand over his face, and it occurred to Webb that he wasn't as much in control as he appeared.

'I wanted a word with all of you as soon as possible, really just to see if you could shed any light on what's happened.'

'Positively none. It's – unbelievable. How anyone –' He broke off.

'Your father didn't mention any problems – disagreements with anyone, which might have led to resentment?'

'Not to me. The last time I saw him was at his birthday party, and no serious topics came up. He said he'd met you for lunch.'

Webb nodded, and Tim continued awkwardly, 'I know you and Dad were old friends. It meant a great deal to him.'

'To me, too.' Webb cleared his throat. 'Did you get the impression he was worried about anything, putting on a brave face for the party, perhaps?'

'Not worried, exactly, but there wasn't much spark about him. After Mum died it slowly began to come back, but then it disappeared again.' He glanced at Webb from beneath his brows. 'I wondered about his marriage; he'd never have discussed it with us, but Jane found them having a row a couple of nights later.'

'You don't care for your stepmother?'

'Can't stand her,' Tim said frankly. 'Poor old Dad – he wouldn't have had much "tender loving care" from that one.

113

If she'd only been home with him, as she should have been, this would never have happened.'

'That's a bit sweeping,' Webb felt impelled to protest. 'It would only hold true if it had been a random attack, a chance break-in.'

Tim looked at him closely. 'And you don't think it was?'

'To be honest, I don't know what the hell I think. We're having to feel our way slowly on this one, and it goes against the grain. Everyone's so strung up, we have to guard against haring off in the wrong direction in our anxiety to nail someone.'

Tim nodded and surreptitiously glanced at his watch. Webb stood up. 'We mustn't take up any more of your time.'

'You'll keep in touch, won't you? Let me know how things are going?'

'Of course. And don't worry, Tim, we'll get him, however long it takes.'

That evening, at the suggestion of the Assistant Chief Constable, Webb was interviewed on regional television, grateful for the presence of the media liaison officer, who kept the questioners in check.

As he gave the carefully worded answers, he'd the uncanny feeling that somewhere out there, in front of one of the thousands of sets tuned to the programme, the killer was also watching and listening. Webb hoped grimly that he would have a sleepless night.

9

Webb had assigned the following morning to interviewing Lethbridge CID, together with those in uniform who'd had contact with Bennett. First, though, he put a call through to the Crown Prosecution Service and was connected with a solicitor by the name of Terence Ryan.

'DCI Webb, Mr Ryan, from Shillingham. I just wanted to let you know I'm investigating the death of Chief Inspector Bennett.'

He waited while the solicitor murmured his condolences.

'Thanks. We have a rather tricky situation here, which I thought you should know about.' Quickly, he outlined the omission from Una's alibi and the unusually long time her journey to Steeple Bayliss had taken, thereby allowing for her having left home later than she'd claimed.

'It might be nothing,' he ended, 'but I thought it was as well to contact you, in case we suddenly need the weight of the law behind us. I'll keep in touch.'

As he put the phone down it started to ring and he lifted it again. It was a call from the house in Westwood Avenue.

'A woman's just turned up, Guv,' the Scenes-of-Crime man informed him. 'Says she's the cleaning lady. She's heard about the murder, and didn't know if she was expected to come in as usual.'

'Right, Phil, thanks; I'm glad she's surfaced – we were wanting a word. Hang on to her and I'll send a couple of men along.' He paused. 'How much longer will you be there?'

'We've all but finished. Should be out by lunchtime.'

Webb put down the phone and lifted the intercom,

wondering whether Una Bennett would now return home. No doubt it would suit Barbara Wood if she did.

Having arranged for Mrs Jones to be interviewed, he began his delicate task.

None of the officers he interviewed had anything but praise for their dead colleague – which, though understandable, did not rule out the possibility that one of them had killed him. Particular attention was paid to anyone Bennett had disciplined recently, but he'd been an easy-going man, not given to draconian punishments, and it seemed unlikely Webb would find a lead there.

Brian Stratton, seen in his turn, volunteered the information that Bennett had seemed particularly low on the morning after his birthday.

'We arrived for work at the same time, and he was looking very down in the mouth. I kidded him about having a hangover.'

'He didn't say what was wrong?'

'No, I wish now I'd probed a bit deeper, but I didn't like to. Malcolm was a private chap, and he'd had his share of worries over the years.'

'Have you met Mrs Bennett?'

Stratton grinned. 'Association of ideas? I've met her a couple of times, but she's not one for joining in social gatherings. Different from his first wife as chalk and cheese – but you'd know that yourself.' He paused. 'Do you still think the killer gained entry by conventional means?'

'It seems that way, certainly, though he was canny enough to break the glass from the outside. In fact, it was something Mrs Bennett said that strengthened the theory, though it might not amount to anything.'

'What was that?'

'She popped back to the house on Saturday for something she'd forgotten, arriving just before one. Simply went in, collected it, and was on her way out again when, as she put it, she had the feeling she was not alone. Even called out for Malcolm, apparently, but no sign of him.'

Stratton frowned. 'So?'

'The point is, she glanced into the kitchen, and if there'd

been glass on the floor at that stage, she'd certainly have seen it. Now, I wouldn't put her down as a fanciful woman, would you? So if she was right, and someone *was* already there, presumably waiting for Malcolm, he *didn't* get in by breaking the glass in the door. That was done later, to make it look like a burglary. Which fits in with the Super's contention that Malc wouldn't have gone on sitting peacefully in his chair while someone knocked hell out of his back door.'

'So the big question is, how did this mysterious person get into the house?'

Webb shrugged helplessly. 'Ask me another. SOCO say there's no sign of locks being forced, either on doors or windows. Perhaps he just said, "Open, bloody Sesame".'

'You've scrubbed the idea that Malcolm could have met the killer and taken him home?'

'I haven't scrubbed anything, Brian. Una's "feeling" could have been just that after all. Let's take a look at the cases Malcolm was involved with during the last month or two.'

Poring over Bennett's notes and files took up the rest of the morning. Stratton had just left him and Webb was preparing to go to lunch when Carter knocked at the door.

'Come in, Jeff. How was Mrs Jones?'

'A nosey little woman, if you ask me, sir. I'm willing to bet she knew damn well she'd not be wanted today; just wanted to boast about being at the murder house.'

'She'd already been there,' Webb pointed out.

'Ah, but she hadn't seen the SOCOs in their overshoes and masks. Her eyes were out on stalks, I can tell you.'

Webb said drily, 'I gather she didn't make a favourable impression.'

'Oh, she was all right. You can't blame her for being curious.'

'She's not been working for them long, has she?'

'Only a couple of weeks, she says, Tuesdays and Fridays. But she told us she won't feel safe there any more. It's my bet she'll be handing in her notice.'

'Poor Mrs Bennett. I hope for her sake SOCO have tidied the place up. Did this Jones woman make any comments about the family?'

'I tried to draw her on that one, but without luck. She only saw the governor once, and that was last week, when she arrived early and he was finishing his breakfast. Come to that, she's not seen much of his wife, either. As soon as she arrives, Mrs Bennett goes off to work.'

'Was the vacancy advertised?'

'I suppose so, but it's pure chance she ever heard of it. It seems the previous cleaner's husband was talking in the pub, saying they were moving up north and joking about how he'd had to behave himself while his wife worked at the Bennetts'. Mrs Jones's son overheard him, and knowing his mother was looking for work, passed it on.'

'OK, Jeff, thanks.' As the sergeant left the room, Webb pulled the phone towards him and dialled Una's office number.

'Sorry to come back to you, Mrs Bennett, but we've just interviewed your cleaner.'

He could almost hear Una's frown. 'What on earth for?'

'She arrived at the house, wondering if she was expected as usual.' He paused. 'When you engaged her, had you advertised the post?'

'Of course.'

'Did you have many replies?'

'One or two, but Mrs Jones was the first and she had good references. She seemed anxious to have the job – spun me a hard-luck story about being a widow with a son on the dole – and since I hadn't time to interview a stream of women, I was glad to settle with her.'

'I see. Well, the men have finished at the house now. You're free to move back whenever you like.'

There was a slight pause, then she said, 'Thank you.'

'The men should have left everything tidy, but you might like Mrs Jones to go in anyway.' Not his place to say she was thinking of giving notice. A thought struck him. 'Has she got a key?'

'No, I wait until she arrives, and she pulls the front door to when she leaves – it has a Yale lock. Thank you, Chief Inspector, I'll get in touch with her.'

*   *   *

118

Una replaced the phone and sat staring at it. She could go home. The thought brought an involuntary shudder. Her stay at Barbara's had been a strain for both of them, but at least she'd had company, and it was so much more convenient, being back in Shillingham.

As the thought came, she realized that, without being aware of it, she had already decided to sell the house and move back here, find somewhere small and suitable like she'd had before her marriage.

The prospect brought a measure of comfort, of which she was instantly ashamed. For behind it lay an unacknowledged desire to shake off all remnants of her marriage as though it had never been – and this even before her husband's funeral and the arrest of his murderer.

And yet, she reflected bleakly, it would have been better for everyone if the marriage never *had* been. Better for Malcolm, for Barbara, for the family – and much better for herself. For a short time it had seemed, miraculously, that her isolation was over, that she could have not only a husband but a ready-made family as well. She'd been a fool to think it would last.

But she should have tried harder, she thought, twisting her pen in her fingers. In Scotland, at the beginning, they'd been happy – there was no denying that. What had gone wrong? Was it her fault?

Yes, she acknowledged painfully; very largely, it was she who'd been to blame. Malcolm had bent over backwards to be accommodating, to help her make the transition. He had allowed her to alter the house that had been his home for twenty years, throwing out his first wife's possessions, redecorating, refurbishing, without a murmur of protest – though his family had more than made up for his forbearance. As she should have anticipated; the house might be more attractive now, but it wouldn't feel like their home. She should have given them time to accept her before embarking on such changes, gone about them gradually.

So Malcolm had given her her head, but what concessions had she made? None. The word dropped into her mind like a pebble in a pool and she moved uncomfortably. Looking back, she saw that she'd consistently refused to alter her schedule, whether at work or the choral society, even when it meant missing police functions which were important to Malcolm, and which his wife was expected to attend. She had let him down all along the line, and, now that she realized the extent of her shortcomings, she was denied the chance to apologize.

The enormity of her guilt was a physical pain. How could she have been so narrow-minded, so entirely self-orientated? He was a good man, fair, kind, considerate. He had offered her everything he had, and she had taken it, giving nothing but her occasional presence in return. No wonder his family hated her. Perhaps, at the end, he had hated her himself.

She put her hands to her face, drawing down the skin under her clutching fingers. Must she live with this for the rest of her life? She'd heard bereavement always brought a sense of guilt, but seldom can that guilt have been more justified. If only she could put the clock back two years and start again!

A knock on the door brought her back to her surroundings. Slowly she lowered her hands and clasped them on the desk.

'Come in,' she said.

Oakacre was a small development off Fenton Street, which had been completed only during the last twelve months. It was a complex of mixed housing, catering for the elderly retired, young married couples and single people. Webb resented it as yet another encroachment on the open land which had surrounded the town when he was a boy. He'd played football here, he thought nostalgically as Jackson turned into the estate.

A parade of shops, new since his last visit, had already closed for the day, and Webb glanced at his watch. Six o'clock.

'Number fifteen,' he said. 'Should be further along on the left.'

They drew in to the kerb and walked up the short path. The door was opened by a fresh-faced girl with dark hair, who looked at them inquiringly.

'We'd like to see Jane Bennett,' Webb said, holding up his warrant card. 'Is she at home?'

120

The girl looked faintly alarmed. 'Yes, she's just got back. Come in.'

The hall was small and square and filled with the aroma of cooking cheese. Jane herself, hearing voices, appeared in a doorway and, recognizing Webb, started forward.

'You've found him? The man who killed Daddy?'

'Not yet, I'm afraid, but we'd like another word with you in the meantime.'

With an apologetic glance at her friend, Jane led the way into the living-room and waved them to a chair. 'What is it?'

'We interviewed Steven Clark yesterday,' Webb said, cautiously lowering himself on to the sagging cushions.

Jane bit her lip, her eyes dropping. 'Yes, he told me.'

Webb was surprised. 'You're still seeing him?'

'No – that is, not really, but he waited for me yesterday, outside work.'

'Why?'

'He said he wanted me to go back to him, that he missed me, and that he was sorry about Dad. He was – quite nice.'

'Will you go?'

She shook her head.

'Jane, he seemed to think you might have told us something about him. What would that have been?'

She flushed. 'I don't know.'

'I think you do,' Webb said, 'and I also think that's the real reason he waited for you. To warn you he might have let something slip.'

She looked at him uncertainly. 'Do I have to tell you? It's nothing to do with Dad, really.'

'But he's mixed up in something, isn't he? Something illegal?'

When she didn't reply, he went on, 'Look, Jane, I'll be straight with you. I'm wondering whether, if he's less than honest, he might know something about the shop-raiding gang, which' – he raised his voice to cover her protest – 'your father was looking into when he died.'

She stared at him in horror. 'You think Steve was connected with my father's death? No! No, no no!'

'We're looking into everyone in any way linked with the

cases he'd been dealing with during the last month or so. We know the gang consists of at least four young men. If Steven moves in dubious circles, he might know who they are, even if he's not personally involved.'

She said in a low voice, 'What he told me isn't anything to do with that.'

'But it *is* dishonest?'

She did not reply. Webb sighed and manoeuvred himself to his feet. 'Very well, we can't force you to cooperate. I just thought that with your father –'

'That's not fair!' she broke in, her eyes filling with tears.

Webb stood looking at her for a moment. Then he said heavily, 'No, it wasn't. I'm sorry.' And, nodding to Jackson to follow him, he walked out of the house.

'What do you make of that then, Guv?' Jackson asked as they reached the car.

'I doubt if we'll get much more out of her. Misguided loyalty – or a touch of the Bennett stubbornness. Either way, it means stalemate. So, Ken, before we knock off for the day we'll pop round to Dick Lane. Young Clark should be home by now and we might be able to twist his arm. Metaphorically speaking,' he added with a tired grin, as Jackson started the car.

As they turned into Dick Lane, Webb instructed, 'Park well before the flat, Ken. Even though the car's unmarked, we don't want to arouse suspicion or he might simply not open the door.'

They drove past the comprehensive school, closed and deserted for the night, and the newsagent's shop where the break-in had occurred.

'Bit close to home, if he was involved in that,' Jackson commented, with a sidelong glance at the drawn blinds.

Webb grunted. 'This'll do. We'll walk the rest of the way.'

The approach to number fifty-nine was less than inviting. The gate had been removed some time in the past – possibly for munitions during the war – and a weed-clogged path led to a drab door from which most of the paint had peeled. Beside it was a row of three bells but, Webb was glad to note, no sign of an intercom, which would have forced them to reveal their identity. He pressed the one marked *Clark*.

When, minutes later, Steven Clark himself opened the door, his reaction was considerably more dramatic than they'd anticipated. After an initial gasp, he tried to slam the door on them, forestalled by Jackson with a well-placed shoe.

'Good evening, Mr Clark,' Webb said pleasantly. 'Time for another chat.' He was interested to see the colour drain out of the young man's face.

Clark swallowed convulsively. 'It's not convenient,' he stammered. 'Tomorrow, I'll be glad –'

'Shall we go up?' Webb continued, as though he hadn't spoken, and moved firmly inside.

Again Clark took them by surprise. He turned and ran to the foot of the stairs, shouting, 'Tony – look out, it's the cops!'

Swiftly, Jackson pushed him aside and ran up the linoleumed steps to the first floor. Webb, mindful of the temptation of the open door, took the precaution of keeping hold of Clark's sleeve as they followed in his wake.

To the right of the stairhead was an open door from which, presumably, Clark had emerged to answer the bell. In the middle of the room thus open to their gaze, another young man stood frozen in panic, his white face turned towards them, his eyes staring. That he had not had time to heed his friend's warning was obvious; the floor was littered with cardboard boxes similar to those Clark had been unpacking when they'd visited him at the supermarket. One, torn open, appeared to be full of cigarette packets. At a rough calculation, there must be several hundred pounds' worth of goods in the room.

'Setting up in opposition, are we?' Webb inquired, then, since no reply was forthcoming, 'Can you offer any explanation for the presence of these goods in your flat?'

Silence.

He fixed his eyes on the second man. 'Name and address?'

It took two attempts before his voice emerged: 'Tony Cooch, one hundred and eleven, Station Road.'

'Very well, I'm arresting you both on suspicion of handling stolen goods. You don't have to say anything, but it may harm your defence if you don't mention when questioned something which you later rely on in court. Anything you do say may be given in evidence.'

Webb turned away and spoke into his mobile phone, arranging for someone to come and collect the goods. Then, having shepherded the young men downstairs, along the pavement and into the car, they drove back to Carrington Street.

This, doubtless, was the scam Jane had stumbled on. Whether or not it had anything to do with the shop raids remained to be seen.

Dean slouched in front of the television, a plate balanced on his knee and a can of beer within reach. Since Sharon had dumped him, this was invariably how he spent his evenings.

His mother was at bingo again, and though he'd never admit it, he no longer felt comfortable alone in the house. Dark and secretive, it lay in wait beyond the lighted room, full of unexplained creaks and movements. Which was why the volume on the set was turned up, even though it was a programme that held no interest for him. Uselessly, he wished he'd brought back a video.

He'd had the dream again last night, and his palms grew wet as, despite his efforts to block it, it surged back into his mind. He'd been hiding in the broom cupboard, heart thundering, while the woman's footsteps ran up the stairs above him and then back down again. And had jumped violently at her sudden call, close at hand: 'Malcolm! Are you there?'

Up to that point, though in all conscience frightening enough, it was no more than what had actually happened; but then the dream became surreally macabre. The handle of the broom cupboard slowly turned, the door opened, and the copper stood there, swaying, blood pouring from his cracked head. And as Dean stared at him in horror, he stretched out a hand as though to touch him. Frantically he had slammed the door, trapping the hand, which was left waggling inside the cupboard with him, the ring glowing on one finger . . .

Dean jumped up, his plate falling unnoticed to the floor as he ran a hand through his sweat-drenched hair. Then, as his breathing steadied, he felt in his pocket for the ring and drew it out, its oddly speckled stone smooth, its goldness warm from his body. Perhaps there was a curse on it, he thought, like stealing from a Pharaoh's tomb; he'd taken it on impulse, as a trophy, but in the succeeding days it had turned into a fetish. As long as he had the ring with him, no harm could befall him. He knew it was ridiculous, but he couldn't shake himself of the idea.

The upturned plate caught his eye, and the food scattered on the carpet. Stuffing the ring back into his pocket, he clumsily knelt to clear it up.

Another thing, he thought uneasily, putting the plate on the table: he didn't want to do that hit tomorrow. His instinct was to lie low until some of the panic about the cop's death had died down, but of course he couldn't tell the others that. He *had* protested it was too soon – only a week since the last raid – and Gary and Wayne had backed him up. The trouble was, Kev needed the buzz. He insisted the fuzz were too busy chasing their tails looking for the cop-killer to waste time on them.

The cop-killer – but that was *him*! Dean felt a thrill of pride, tempered with fear. One day, perhaps, when the heat had died down, he'd tell them. In the meantime, tomorrow loomed ever nearer. They'd decided on Dring's in King Street, mid-afternoon, when it was quiet. Kev was sounding out Tony and Steve for some tips; working at Savemore, they'd know the form.

So Kev would get his fix and he, too, would experience that potent draught of fear and excitement. Though nothing in the world, he told himself, could compare with the triumph he'd felt as he'd cracked down on that lousy copper and battered the rotten life out of him. Justice had been done. He just wished he didn't keep dreaming about it.

He picked up the beer can and held it up to his reflection in the mirror. 'Tomorrow!' he toasted aloud, and, tipping back his head, poured its contents down his throat.

'So by the time we got that lot sorted, it was after eight before I got back. I've only just finished my meal.'

Hannah said, 'Do you think they've anything to do with the shop raids?'

'At this stage, it's anybody's guess. You may rest assured they'll be thoroughly questioned.'

'And Malcolm's daughter was involved with one of them?'

'Yep. His instincts were right – he told me he didn't like Jane's young man. I'll have to question her again, of course; there could be a charge of withholding information, but I have the feeling that as soon as she discovered what he was up to, she upped and left him. Anyway, enough of all that; can I freshen your drink?'

'Thanks.' Hannah leaned back in the chair, looking round the pleasant, masculine room. It was a second home to her, with its oak furniture, deep, comfortable chairs and the cinnamon-coloured walls on which David's favourite paintings hung.

She watched him as he poured the drinks. This case was taking a lot out of him, and they were only a few days into it. She was worried about him, which was why she'd come upstairs a few minutes ago, though she'd brought a book on art with her as an excuse.

'I happened to see it in the library, and thought it might interest you,' she'd told him, and he had nodded absently and thanked her, laying it down on a table.

'So,' she said now, taking the glass he held out, 'how's the case going?'

Before he could reply, the front-door bell pealed through the flat. Webb raised his eyebrows, laid down his drink and went to answer it. Through the open living-room door, Hannah heard a woman's voice say, 'Hello, Dave. Surprise, surprise!'

She tensed, straining to hear his reply, and the single word – 'Susan!' – confirmed her worst fears. David's ex-wife, that shadowy figure whose going, nine long years ago, had hurt him so deeply, and whose sudden reappearance, more recently, had dealt their own relationship an almost fatal blow.

'Well, aren't you going to ask me in?' she was saying, an edge creeping into her voice.

'Yes – yes, of course.'

Hannah rose slowly to her feet and was facing the door when Susan entered, closely followed by David, mouthing his apologies behind her back.

She stopped on the threshold. 'Am I interrupting something?'

'Not at all,' David said evenly. 'Let me introduce you. This is Hannah James, who lives on the floor below. Hannah, Susan – Farrow. My ex-wife.'

The two women nodded warily at each other.

'Miss James kindly brought me an art book to look at, and stayed for a drink,' David added lamely.

Which, Hannah thought, neatly demoted her to an importunate neighbour. Was that what he wanted Susan to believe? If so, he was to be disappointed. She said abruptly, 'Are you the schoolteacher?'

Hannah raised an eyebrow. 'I do teach, yes.'

Having established her identity, Susan turned back to David, still standing uncertainly at her side.

'I just couldn't believe it – about Malcolm.'

'I know; it's grim.'

'I only realized you were in charge when I saw you on TV. How can you do it, when you were such friends?'

He said woodenly, 'I can't pick and choose my cases. Would you like a drink?'

'Yes, please – the usual. Then I want to hear all about it.' She seated herself in David's chair and sat back, crossing her legs.

Hannah put her glass on the table. 'I must be going, so if you'll excuse me –'

David said quickly, 'Sit down, Hannah; you haven't finished your drink.'

'Another time,' she answered brightly. 'I hope you enjoy the book.' She turned briefly to the seated woman. 'Nice to have met you, Mrs Farrow.' And before either of them could speak, she walked quickly out of the room.

Her feelings as she ran back down the stairs were chaotic, and, letting herself into her flat, she tried to sort them out. Susan was back. *Was* she still a threat? She was an attractive

127

woman, Hannah conceded, tall and boyishly slim, her flaxen hair in a soft bob, her eyes blue. But it was her mouth that held the attention; her teeth, though even and well-shaped, were positioned too far forward, with the result that when her lips closed over them, they looked full and disturbingly sensual.

This had been Hannah's first chance of a proper look at her; the only other time she'd seen Susan was that brief, heart-stopping moment when she and David had come down the stairs from his flat early one morning, just as, in her dressing-gown, Hannah was opening her own door to take in the milk.

She walked restlessly into the lamplit sitting-room. The clock on the mantelpiece showed nine-thirty; an odd hour to call on one's ex-husband. Would she see them coming down the stairs tomorrow morning?

Pushing the thought from her mind, Hannah sat on the sofa, reached for a glossy magazine and mechanically started turning its pages. At ten o'clock the doorbell rang and she went to answer it.

David came swiftly in, pushed the door shut with his foot, and took her in his arms, holding her tightly.

'Hey!' she exclaimed with a breathless little laugh. 'What's all this about?'

He said against her hair, 'I needed to see you.'

'Why?'

'To reassure myself that you're still here, that we're still us. Seeing Susan sitting there brought back all the trauma of those years we were together and frankly, what with Malcolm's death and everything, I'm not up to it.'

'Has she gone?'

'Yes, and she won't be back, love. I made a fool of myself once, and look how long it took me to get you back again! I'm not likely to make the same mistake twice.'

'I'm glad to hear it!' she said with mock severity, a deep well of thankfulness inside her. 'What did she mean,' she added as they walked back to the sitting-room, his arm still round her, 'was I "the schoolteacher"?'

'I must have mentioned you, last time. Look, love, she only

came to find out about Malcolm. As you know, we were all good friends, years ago.'

'Yes, of course,' Hannah said.

'So if it's all the same to you, how about finishing that interrupted drink?'

And, dismissing her doubts, Hannah smilingly complied.

10

Sally lowered the baby into his bouncing chair and glanced at her husband.

'Aren't you going to be late? It's after eight-thirty.'

He didn't look up from the paper. 'I've got a man coming to see the Merc at nine. Only time he could manage it. Still, I've an appointment with a client later, so it fits in quite well.'

'I didn't know you'd actually advertised it.'

'I haven't, it's the friend of a friend.'

Sally sat down and reached for the toast. Neil's financial problems had not been mentioned for the last two weeks; her father's death had put them completely out of her mind and Neil himself had volunteered nothing. Even now, she was reluctant to bring the subject up, knowing the friction that would result.

She said tentatively, 'Is – everything working out?'

He shrugged, still behind the paper. 'I'm seeing the bank manager this afternoon. I'll tell you after that.'

She buttered the toast, letting the matter drop. It occurred to her that if she received anything from her father's estate, Neil would assume a share in it. But she'd no intention of seeing her legacy disappear as money tended to do when he got his hands on it. It might be wise to speak to someone – an accountant – and see if she could tie it up in some way, perhaps as a trust fund for Jamie. Still, no point in worrying about that yet; for all she knew, Dad might have left everything to Una.

Una. Broodingly, Sally thought about her stepmother. Barbara'd phoned last night to say the police had moved out of the house and Una would be going back today. It occurred to

Sally that neither she nor Tim had seen their stepmother since the murder, and Jane only by accident, when she called at Barbara's. Which, she thought guiltily, was unforgivable. She would make a point of going round this evening, though the prospect filled her with dread. Being in the familiar house without Dad would be bad enough, let alone the strain of offering condolences to Una, with no idea how they'd be received.

She said aloud, 'Una's moving back home today, did I tell you?'

Neil merely grunted.

'I thought I'd go round this evening and see how she is. Take her some flowers, perhaps.'

'Bit of a change of heart, isn't it?'

'Like it or not, we're all she's got now. Anyway, Dad would have wanted me to.'

'Why not go this morning, then, and get it over, instead of disrupting our evening?'

'Because she'll be at work; she went back on Monday.'

He looked up then. '*Monday*? My God, she's as hard as nails, that one.'

'It probably helped take her mind off things. I do wish we could hold the funeral,' she added unsteadily. 'This waiting around is horrible, like being in limbo.'

'I suppose they need to find out who did it, before they can release the body.'

Sally shuddered. 'Who *could* have done it, Neil? Who'd want to hurt Dad?'

'Some yobbo with a grudge against him, no doubt.'

'But in that case, surely he'd have been attacked outside somewhere? Why at home?'

'Because he was quite literally a sitting target.'

'But no one could have known that in advance. And how did whoever it was get into the house?'

Neil folded his paper. 'I still think he must have met someone on the way home.'

'He'd never have invited a "yobbo" into the house.'

'He could have forced his way in.'

131

'In which case, Dad wouldn't have given him the opportunity to creep up on him.'

'Hell, Sally, I don't know; I'm not a detective. Go and ask your pal Webb.' With which he pushed back his chair and left the room.

The baby was beginning to grizzle and, bending down, Sally lifted him out of his bouncer. With her mother and father dead and her husband increasingly unapproachable, this tiny child was becoming her only anchor. She held him close, laying her face against his soft cheek. Together, she promised him silently, they would survive.

In fact, had Sally gone to Lethbridge straight away, she would have found Una at home. After an early breakfast she had packed her suitcase, thanked Barbara for her hospitality, and driven over, ostensibly to let in Mrs Jones. However, she was also anxious that her first return to the house should not be in darkness; it would have been too reminiscent of the last time she'd come home.

Even so, she had to brace herself as she turned into Westwood Avenue and drew up outside the house. It looked so exactly the same, with no hint of the horrendous event that had taken place there. The grass that Malcolm had given its first cut only last week lay as he had left it, its edges neatly trimmed. She remembered him whistling as he worked, the ease with which he wielded the heavy implements. If his killer had faced him squarely, it would have taken a strong man to fell him.

Una stopped suddenly on the path, aware with a slight sense of shock that it had never occurred to her to wonder who that killer was. Malcolm's working life had been a closed book to her, and she'd merely assumed that something connected with it had led to his death.

Now, she registered for the first time that the killer had known where he lived; was that because he knew Malcolm socially, or simply that he'd followed him home? Neither alternative was particularly palatable.

She let herself into the house and stood in the square hallway, shivering. Then, steeling herself, she went into the sitting-room. It looked strangely alien, its furniture slightly out of alignment and odd signs here and there of the four-day police presence. Icy cold, she walked, as she had the last time, round Malcolm's chair, still in its usual position, and forced herself to stare down at it, while memory painted in the slumped figure of her dead husband. The back cushions seemed slightly damp; no doubt they'd been scrubbed to remove traces of blood.

She said aloud, 'Oh Malcolm, who did this to you?' – and started violently as a knock sounded on the back door.

She went through to the kitchen. The glass pane in the door had not yet been replaced, and a piece of hardboard was nailed across the gap, making the room unusually dark. With hands that shook, she unlocked the door and stepped aside as Mrs Jones came into the house.

The woman darted a furtive look at her. 'Oh, Mrs Bennett, I don't know what to say!'

'It's all right, Mrs Jones. By the way, please don't worry about the – the sitting-room. The police cleared everything up, it only needs its usual clean.'

The woman nodded, hanging up her coat to reveal the flowered apron.

'I couldn't believe it, when I saw it in the papers! I only saw Mr Bennett on Friday! There he was' – she gestured at the kitchen table – 'as large as life, eating his breakfast! And to think,' she added with morbid relish, 'that he had only one more day left to him!'

Una said hastily, 'I must be on my way, Mrs Jones. I've moved back here now, so I'll see you on Friday as usual.'

The woman hesitated. 'Well, I – '

'Perhaps I should mention that as soon as the legal formalities are complete, I'll be putting the house on the market – it's too big for me to stay here alone. However, I'd be very grateful if you'd stay on till the sale goes through.'

Mrs Jones twisted her apron in her hands. 'I'll be honest with you, Mrs Bennett. I don't feel – comfortable working here any more. In fact – I won't lie to you – I was going to give in my notice today.' She darted another quick glance at

Una's graven face. 'How – how long would it be, like, before you sell the house?'

'Several months, I suppose. But if I find somewhere that suits me in the meantime, I should probably move out then.'

'Well, I don't like to let you down, like, in your present state and all. Say I stay on for a few weeks, and see how it goes?'

'I'd appreciate that. Thank you. Now, I really must be going.' Una picked up her handbag and, with a brief smile, hurried from the house.

On the way back to Shillingham, she was perturbed to discover tears raining down her face. She made no attempt to analyse them, simply kept brushing them away so that she could see clearly enough to drive. But she was realizing that when she returned home this evening there would be no warm smell of dinner to greet her, no one to come forward with a smile and a kiss to ask how her day had gone. Oh Malcolm, she thought desolately, why didn't I value you when I had you?

Carter said, 'Sir, you know the name "Kev" came up on that shop raid?'

Webb nodded, remembering his conversation with Malcolm in the pub.

'Well, we might have a lead there. Routine inquiries have come up with one Kevin Baker. Couple of convictions for burglary. He's moved from the address we had, but word is he frequents the Oliver Cromwell in Market Street. I thought me and Frear could go along this evening, see if we can sniff him out.'

'Good idea, Jeff. Any known associates?'

'He used to hang round with Gary Higgs. Don't know if they're still mates.'

'We're looking for a foursome; still, gangs break up and re-form, as we know. Any history of violence?'

'Not on record, sir.'

'I suppose there's always a first time. It would be good to nab them for the raids, but I doubt if there's any connection with the murder; if Baker used a knife at the shop, he'd have gone for the same method again. Still, no harm in giving them a once-over. You heard about the two lads we collared yesterday?'

'Yes, sir. Did they cough?'

'I didn't stay for the interviews, but I've asked DS Partridge to keep us informed. In fact, we'd gone to see Clark in connection with Mr Bennett's death; the discovery of the loot was a bonus.'

Carter said diffidently, 'Isn't he Jane Bennett's boyfriend?'

'He was; we wondered if he blamed the DCI for Jane leaving. Having met him, I doubt if he's a killer, but we're going through all the motions.'

Noting the sergeant's anxious expression, he added, 'She ditched him because she suspected something wasn't kosher. Don't worry, Jeff, nothing can rub off on Jane.'

'That's a relief. She's got enough to cope with at the moment.'

'It's just possible,' Webb continued, 'that if Clark and his buddy mix in shady company, they might have heard something about the raids. That's what we're hoping, anyway. They couldn't have been personally involved, because they both work full time at Savemore's. At least, they were doing up to now; I doubt if they'll be there much longer, once the management gets wind of their racket.' He glanced at his watch. 'In fact, you could give Partridge a ring and see if anything useful came up.'

'Right, sir.'

'You've not had any more thoughts about who might have a grudge against Mr Bennett?'

'Not really, no. We've been through all his cases for the last two or three months, and I shouldn't think anything older would be relevant.'

'Nothing promising?'

'Well, obviously several villains went to jail during that time, and could have held the governor responsible. There was Blackie Moore, for instance, but he seemed to take his sentencing quite philosophically. And the Smithson gang. They muttered various imprecations, but that's par for the course. All the same, their associates are being rounded up.

135

And the chap who topped himself in jail – he was one of the guv's collars, too, but he was a loner. No one to avenge him.'

Carter hesitated. 'Personally, sir, I'm beginning to doubt if it was anything to do with the job. If it was, why didn't they lie in wait for him somewhere? Why hit him at home? Seems much more likely to be a civilian matter, to me.'

'They could have followed him when he left the station. He always walked home – they could easily have found out where he lived.'

'But on a Saturday afternoon? Surely everyone would expect his family to be at home?'

Webb sat back, staring down at the desk reflectively. 'What are you saying, Jeff? That you think it was a spur-of-the-moment thing? Unpremeditated, by someone he knew socially?'

'It's a possibility, at least.'

'Well, the family have already given us a list of all the friends and acquaintances they could think of. I'll get on to them again, see if they can come up with any more.'

Carter said hesitantly, 'There's always the family themselves.'

'Most murders being domestic?' Webb asked with a wry grin.

Carter flushed. 'Sorry, sir, I'm not trying to teach you to suck eggs. It's just that that son-in-law's an odd bloke. Like I said, he was in here seeing Mr Bennett, and the guv was quite upset when he left, snapping at everyone, which wasn't like him.'

'He was after a loan, apparently. I've seen him, of course, but I did make a note to go back.'

'There's no possibility the wife could have done it?'

'Oh, there's a possibility, all right; the timing is crucial, and it *did* take her a long time to get to SB. She said it was because of hold-ups on the way, but she's not been entirely ruled out.'

He looked up at Carter under his brows. 'Nor has anyone here, in the station. There could be someone who didn't see eye to eye with Mr Bennett, resented his popularity.'

The sergeant was silent, but Webb could feel the wall of his resistance, his refusal even to consider that one of his colleagues might be responsible. Webb understood, but it was imperative to keep an open mind.

'OK, Jeff, you go and ring Don Partridge and I'll see if I can jog the family's memories a bit more.'

Carter nodded and left the room. Webb rubbed his hands over his face. This was proving the devil of a case, as was only to be expected. Still, it wouldn't be solved by sitting here brooding about it. He pushed back his chair and went in search of Jackson.

Unlike Una, Barbara wondered constantly about the murderer's identity. Malcolm had sometimes spoken to her of cases he was involved with, sensing her genuine interest in his work, which, she suspected, Una did not share. Was the attack something she should have foreseen? Could she, if she'd intervened somehow, have prevented it?

Lying awake night after night, there were few people of her acquaintance whom she had not tried out in the guise of murderer, though by the light of day such suppositions seemed ludicrous.

Nevertheless, she was aware that this constant worrying at the problem helped keep at bay the agony of loss which, in public, she was forced to conceal. She'd discovered, though, that Malcolm's death had in some way removed the restraints which, even in private, she'd always imposed on her thoughts of him. In her mind, she talked to him constantly, claiming him as her love as she could never have done while he lived.

My darling! she thought now in a wave of anguish. Oh, my darling! Did you know, in that last moment, what was happening? And *why*?

Out in the corridor, a bell sounded for the end of break. Barbara realized she'd been sitting here since the last lesson ended, and had missed her coffee. She must be more careful; Miss James had been understanding about her breakdown, and to her shame she'd offered the reminder of Carol's death

137

as an explanation. She did not, however, wish her conduct to become a matter of comment in the staff-room.

She straightened her back, sorted out the papers in front of her, and by the time the next class arrived, was fully in control again. Life, she thought bitterly, must go on.

A few streets away, Jane was having less success in hiding her feelings. Her lengthy absence from her computer having been noted, one of the girls was dispatched to look for her, and found her in floods of tears in the cloakroom.

Mary Telford, a motherly young woman, put her arms round her and Jane continued to sob helplessly in her arms. The whole office knew about Jane's father, and the manager had asked them to give her as much support as possible. Helplessly, Mary wondered what she should do.

'I want him back!' Jane sobbed. 'I just want him back!'

'I know, love. You cry, if it helps.'

'It doesn't.' Jane raised her head and fumbled for her sodden handkerchief. 'First Mum, now Dad. I haven't even got Steve any more,' she added desolately.

'Well,' Mary said, casting round for comfort and privy to office gossip, 'that was your doing, wasn't it, and he's no great loss.'

Jane blew her nose. 'But I might have got him into trouble. I didn't mean to, but the police seemed suspicious of him. They even thought' – she half-choked with indignation – 'that he might have killed Dad!'

Mary gazed at her in shock. 'Steve? He didn't, did he?'

'Of course he didn't. But he was involved in other things, and if they catch him, he'll blame me. He always said I was a real copper's daughter.'

'If he was doing wrong, he was bound to be found out sooner or later,' Mary said severely, 'so don't waste your sympathy on him. Now, if you're feeling a bit better, come back to the office and I'll make a nice cup of coffee. How about that?'

Jane nodded. 'OK. Thanks.'

And, drained by her tears, she meekly followed Mary back to her desk.

11

It was turning out to be a longer lunch break than Una normally allowed herself. Having eaten, she'd called in to see her solicitor, and it was as she was walking back to the office that she paused on impulse at an estate agent's window to study the properties for sale.

Her attention was caught by an attractive-looking cottage on the northern edge of town, and she hesitated. It was farther out than her flat had been, but would not be more than ten minutes' drive at most from the office.

Without any clear-cut intention, she went inside and was immediately ushered to a chair opposite an eager young man.

'Could you give me some details about the cottage in the window?' she asked diffidently. 'The one in North Park?'

'Ah yes, Ginger's.' He flicked through a file on his desk and withdrew a sheet of particulars. 'It only came in yesterday, and I don't think it'll be on the books long – it's a very good price, considering the position.'

No doubt a standard response, Una thought as she noted the accommodation on offer, and since it was still a buyer's market she was not wholly convinced. Meanwhile, the young man – 'Danny', according to the name-plate on his desk – had taken out a card and was asking her exactly what kind of property she was interested in.

Una listed her preferences, finding they crystallized as she considered them, and watched with interest as he withdrew several more sheets from a drawer and passed them across. One or two seemed possibilities, and some were in the centre of town, which she'd really prefer.

'If you're free this afternoon, Mrs Bennett, I could run you over to Ginger's. The owners are away, but we have the key to the property. And if any of the others appeal to you, I can phone and arrange an appointment to view.'

Una felt a lift of excitement, her first positive emotion in four days. The restlessness which had been growing all week made the prospect of an afternoon at her desk suddenly unappealing, and there was nothing urgent awaiting her attention. The brief excursion would do her good, she told herself, as well as giving her some idea of the type of property on sale in her price range.

'Yes,' she replied, 'I'd like to see Ginger's, and perhaps the flat in Hampton Rise, if it's possible.'

'Fine, that one comes with vacant possession – the owner can move out any time. I'll give her a call and see when would be convenient.'

Vacant possession. The words rang temptingly in Una's ears. Perhaps after all she wouldn't have to spend too long alone in Westwood Avenue. All at once, the afternoon ahead seemed full of promise, and, feeling like a truant, she determined guiltily to enjoy it.

Neil's meeting with the bank manager had not gone particularly well; having been called upon to dig him out of similar predicaments in the past, Mr Latimer was not disposed to be obliging, and Neil had had to do a fair amount of begging, which had gone very much against the grain.

In the end, he had gained a little and of necessity agreed to sacrifice a lot, including the car and his membership of the golf club. But at least he was now in a position to repay the money he'd 'borrowed' from the client's account before it was missed, which had been his most urgent worry.

Damn it, he thought, if old Malcolm had to die, it was a pity he hadn't done so a month or two earlier; Sally's share of the proceeds would have seen them over this hiccup.

As the thought registered, he felt himself go hot, wondering if it had also been in Webb's mind. Still, he could think what he liked; the money would soon be in their hands, and with luck something might still be salvaged out of the mess. It was bloody infuriating that he was always hamstrung like this through lack of funds. If he'd had money to play around with, he'd have made a packet by now.

He stood on the pavement outside the bank, brooding on his position and reluctant to return immediately to the bustle of the office. It was Wednesday afternoon, half-day closing for the smaller shops, and the road was unusually quiet.

A sudden commotion a few doors down made him turn, in time to see three hooded youths come running out of the supermarket and into a van waiting at the kerb. As one of them climbed in, he ripped off his hood and stuffed it into his pocket; but in withdrawing his hand, something small and bright fell unnoticed to the ground, winking in the sunlight.

Neil moved forward instinctively. The van started up with a roar, and, as he stooped to retrieve the object, disappeared round the corner into Franklyn Road. In the same moment, a man came running out of the supermarket, shouting, 'Which way did they go? They've got away with our takings!'

'Round the corner,' Neil told him, pointing. 'I didn't get their number, but one of them dropped this.'

But the manager wasn't listening. Seeing a policeman across the road, he waved frantically and shouted, and the officer began to run towards him. Neil stood frowning at the ring in his hand, a gold ring, with a dull green stone. It looked familiar; very similar, he thought suddenly, to that which Una had given Malcolm for his birthday, and which they'd been called on to admire at that disastrous dinner party. But Malcolm's ring hadn't gone missing – had it?

He hesitated. Obviously he must hand the ring over, but first he had to be sure it wasn't Malcolm's. Una's office was just down the road; he'd go and check with her first.

The policeman was now accompanying the manager into the supermarket, and, anxious not to be detained as a witness before he was ready, Neil walked quickly on to Lowther Building and went inside.

Ginger's Cottage had proved interesting, and Una'd enjoyed wandering round it, Danny in tow, imagining her furniture in the different rooms.

There were, however, several drawbacks; the garden was

larger than she wanted, though Danny insisted it would be a simple matter to pave it over and make it into a container garden. Also, the decoration was in a poor state and she suspected there might be damp in a couple of places. Nevertheless, on the drive back to Shillingham she was seriously considering its potential.

Until she saw the flat in Hampton Rise, which also appealed to her. Suddenly, Una found herself in the unexpected position of being spoiled for choice – and this when she hadn't even planned to start house-hunting.

Furthermore, several of the other properties whose details she'd been given sounded promising, and before she parted from Danny, she asked him to arrange appointments to view those as well.

He dropped her, at her request, in Gloucester Circus. It was a quarter past three, and as a fitting end to her truancy, she'd decided to have tea at the King's Head before returning to the office. She wanted to sit quietly and read through the particulars again, both of the places she'd seen and those she hoped to view.

Some forty minutes later, walking back along King Street, she found to her amusement that she was rehearsing explanations of her absence to give the staff. But, damn it, she owned the place! She didn't have to tell anyone anything.

As she was approaching Dring's superstore, a police car drew to a halt outside it and two uniformed men went inside. Someone caught shoplifting, she thought idly as she continued down the road to Lowther Building.

In the foyer, there was an unusual number of people gathered round the lifts. One had been out of service all day, and everyone was looking impatiently up at the illuminated number indicating where the other had stopped.

'Seems to be stuck on the second floor,' someone remarked.

Since she'd wasted enough time that afternoon, Una made her way to the other pair of lifts at the back of the building. She emerged on the second floor at some distance from her office and walked briskly along a corridor and round the corner which would lead her there.

And stopped abruptly. Halfway down the corridor she could

142

see the figure of a man lying on the floor, half in and half out of the lift. Which, she thought, starting to run, would explain why it wasn't responding to the bell. He must have had a heart attack.

Blurred memories of artificial respiration jostled in her mind and, as she reached the prone figure, instantly vanished. For this was no heart-attack victim. He was lying face down and, protruding from the centre of his back, was the handle of a knife.

Without thinking, frantic to help him, Una caught hold of it and tried, unsuccessfully, to pull it free. And in the same moment, the door of her own office opened behind her and she heard someone scream.

'Get help!' she gasped over her shoulder. 'Dial 999!' Abandoning her attempt to free the knife, she bent down, hoping to detect signs of life.

'We're getting help,' she told the inert figure. 'Just –'

Her voice tailed away in horror and, straightening, she backed away, her hand going to her throat. Someone took her arm and Eve Bundy's voice said shakily, 'Miss Drew – are you all right? What happened?'

Una shook her head speechlessly. A girl somewhere over to her left – the one who had screamed – cried hysterically, 'She stabbed him, that's what happened! I saw her! I *saw* her!'

Paralysed with shock, Una heard Rosemary say sharply, 'Don't be ridiculous; why should Miss Drew stab a man she doesn't even now?'

'But I do know him,' Una contradicted through chattering teeth. 'It's my son-in-law, Neil Crawford.'

'*What*?' Webb started up out of his chair. 'When? How?'

He stood listening to the voice over the phone, his face grim. 'OK, Alan, I'll be right over. Thanks.'

He dropped the phone on its cradle, strode into the outer office and beckoned Jackson on his way through it. 'Come on, Ken, back to Shillingham at the double. Neil Crawford's been murdered.'

Jackson hurried after him out of the building and over to

their car in the forecourt. 'We were just going to see him, weren't we, Guv?'

'We still are,' Webb said shortly.

'But –'

'What I didn't say in there was that he was found outside Una Bennett's office, with her standing over him.'

'Never!'

'There's some young girl at the scene who insists she saw her stabbing him. What the hell was Crawford doing there, anyway? He couldn't stand the sight of her.'

'She might have phoned and asked him to call.'

'Then promptly murdered him? Hardly subtle.'

'Perhaps,' Jackson said tentatively, turning the car in the direction of Shillingham, 'he'd found something which linked her with Mr Bennett's death?'

'Well, we've not ruled her out on that, as I was telling Jeff Carter this morning.'

They drove in silence for a while along the familiar country road. Then Jackson asked, 'Where's Mrs Bennett now?'

'At Carrington Street.'

'Under arrest?'

'Helping with inquiries. At the very least, she's a lot of explaining to do.'

'Is that where we're making for, Guv?'

'Not immediately; we'll look at the scene first.'

Having fought their way through the press into Lowther Building, they found a notice in front of the lifts stating that both were out of order, but that others could be found at the rear of the building.

On the second floor, a uniformed constable was waiting to escort them to the Drew offices. As they turned the final corner, they could see the pathologist kneeling on the floor beside the body. To one side, a couple of Scenes-of-Crime men waited for him to complete his examination.

'Death instantaneous, I'd say,' Stapleton remarked as Webb and Jackson came up. He rose to his feet and fastidiously brushed the knees of his trousers. 'Roughly an hour ago.'

Webb glanced at his watch. 'Making it around four?'

'I said "roughly", Chief Inspector. However,' Stapleton permitted himself a thin smile, 'since that was when the body was discovered, and, according to witnesses, still bleeding, I believe I may be fairly precise on this occasion.'

Alan Crombie appeared in the adjacent doorway and, nodding to the pathologist, Webb moved inside with him and followed him into one of the small rooms to the right of the foyer.

'Just to bring you up to date, Dave,' Crombie said, 'we've called in a support team, and they're visiting all the offices in the building, asking when people last used the front lift. Also, if anyone saw either Crawford or Mrs Bennett this afternoon; there's an outside chance someone might have come up in the lift with him, say as far as the first floor.'

'Who claims to have seen the stabbing?'

'A messenger girl from the stationer's in Duke Street. She'd delivered some stuff and when she opened the door to leave, she swears Mrs Bennett was plunging the knife in.'

'Where is she now?'

'In the next room, with Nickie Hunt. I thought you'd want to see her.'

'Any corroborating evidence?'

'The manageress was on the scene almost at once, alerted by her scream. By that time Mrs Bennett was backing away from the body.'

' "By that time", Alan? You believe the girl?'

'I believe *she* believes it.'

'What does Mrs Bennett say?'

'She hasn't said anything yet, in my hearing.'

'Waiting for her solicitor?'

'Simply in shock, I'd say.'

'And the rest of them' – Webb nodded towards the door – 'heard nothing until the scream?'

'No, we've just finished interviewing them. One odd point, though: Mrs Bennett – or Miss Drew, as they call her – didn't come back after lunch. Apparently this is completely unheard-of and had already caused no end of speculation.'

'You mean she left for lunch as usual, and hadn't been seen since?'

'That's right; not until she was "allegedly" found with the knife in her hand.'

'Then where the hell had she been?'

'We've not had a chance to ask her; this didn't come up till after she'd been taken back to the station. Suppose she met Crawford, either by chance or appointment, and they had a row of some kind? He followed her back and into the lift, perhaps still arguing, and in a fit of temper she stabbed him.'

'Happening to have a knife handy for just such an eventuality?'

'Well, she could have, if she'd already topped her husband.'

'Anyway, it's been established that the lift was the scene of crime, rather than the corridor?'

'It seems so, since he was lying half inside it. The hypothesis at the moment is that the murderer came up in the lift with Crawford and stabbed him in the back as he was getting out. The angle of the wound supports that.'

'Or he – or she – could have stabbed him as they ascended, supported him till the door opened, then pushed him out?'

'Same difference.'

'But if the lift was the scene of the crime, and supposing for the moment that Mrs Bennett *was* the killer, why was she "allegedly" still bending over him when the girl saw her? It would have been more prudent to have got the hell out of it.'

'God, Dave, you tell me. By the way, we've taken over this place as an incident room for the moment. Very convenient, as you can see, with everything laid on.'

'How many staff are there?'

'The manageress, the receptionist and six girls. And they're all adamant that Neil Crawford's never been here.'

'Until now.'

'Even now, he never made it inside.'

'Any comments on Mrs Bennett's recent behaviour, apart from skiving off for the afternoon?'

'They were shocked that she came straight back to work on Monday, though not really surprised. She's known as a disciplinarian and is as hard on herself as the staff. There was a row with one of them a couple of weeks ago; harsh things were said, but when she asked to come back, Mrs B let her.'

'She hasn't mentioned Crawford to anyone?'

Crombie shook his head. 'Never discussed her private life.'

The two men moved into the foyer, watching through the open door as the SOCO photographer snapped the body from all angles. The corridor on either side of the lift had already been tested for shoe marks; if the killer were not Una Bennett, he must have made his escape in one direction or the other, since the second lift wasn't working. The likeliest route was through a door farther along, which opened on to a flight of stairs. They, too, were being dusted for prints.

Webb said suddenly, 'Crawford's name hasn't been released yet?'

'No.'

'Family been contacted?'

'Someone's gone to see his wife. I don't know about the rest of them.'

Webb shook his head sadly, thinking of Sally and her baby. He'd have to see her, but he'd leave it till tomorrow, let her get over the initial shock.

'Well, I suppose I'd better see this girl. What's her name?'

'Daisy Saunders. She was a bit hysterical but Nickie's managed to calm her down.' Crombie gestured towards the middle door on the right and Webb, after a brief tap, opened it and went inside. WDC Hunt rose from a chair.

'Good afternoon, sir. This is Daisy Saunders.'

Webb nodded at her, introduced himself, and pulled up a chair. She was in her early twenties, with short, spiky black hair, and she was wearing leather trousers and jacket. A motorcycle helmet lay on the floor beside her. She returned Webb's look dubiously from heavily made-up eyes.

'Now, I'm sure you've been through this already, but I'd like you to tell me exactly what happened here this afternoon.'

She heaved an exaggerated sigh. 'Not again! I've not remembered anything else, you know. There's nothing more *to* remember.'

'Just bear with me, please.'

'Well, like I said, I brought some stationery over and left it

147

with the woman in reception as usual. She signed for it, and I was on my way out when I saw them.' Her voice faltered and she came to a halt.

'Yes?' Webb said encouragingly.

'There was a guy lying on the ground and this woman bending over him with the knife in her hands.'

'*Hands*, Daisy? Both of them?'

'Yeah, both of 'em. Forcing it in.' She shuddered.

'But you didn't actually see her stab him?'

'All but,' she said defiantly.

Webb was silent for a moment, then he asked, 'Did you know who she was?'

'I knew she was a murderer. That was enough for me.'

'You *assumed* she was a murderer,' he corrected. 'But had you seen her before?'

'No, never.'

'Were you surprised to learn it was Mrs – Miss Drew, the owner of the firm?'

'Suppose I was, a bit. But her old man snuffed it last week, didn't he? Must be getting to be a habit.'

'Miss Saunders, I really must warn you against making remarks like that. As yet there's been no –'

'Look, my lover, you can warn me all you like, but I know what I saw, and I'm telling you the knife was in his back and she was holding it. That good enough for you?'

Nickie Hunt moved in embarrassment, avoiding Webb's eye.

He asked impassively, 'What did she do when you screamed? Did she look guilty or frightened?'

'No, she just shouted, "Get help! Dial 999!"'

'It didn't strike you she might just as easily have been trying to pull the knife *out*?'

She stared at him for a moment. Then she said woodenly, 'No, it didn't.'

'But with hindsight, would you say it was possible?'

The girl frowned. 'You mean she might just have found him there?'

'She might, or she might have seen someone else stab him. Suppose, just for a moment, that it was you who found him.

You opened the door and there he was, lying in front of you. No sign of Miss Drew or anyone else. What would you have done? Tried to pull the knife out?'

'Not likely! I'd have done exactly what I done anyway, screamed blue murder.'

Webb smiled slightly, leaning back in his seat. 'Quite right, too. It's very dangerous to remove a knife from a wound – you could do more damage than leaving it in place.'

She said acidly, 'I'll remember that, next time.'

There was a tap on the door and Jackson put his head round it.

'Excuse me, Guv, SOCO have finished and the hearse is waiting.'

Webb got to his feet. 'Thank you, Sergeant.' He turned back to the girl. 'And thank you, Miss Saunders. If you'll call in at Carrington Street Police Station tomorrow, your statement will be typed up. Are you fit to bike back to Duke Street?'

'Oh yeah, ta. I've had some tea and I'm OK now.'

'Very well. Once the body's been removed, you'll be free to go.'

And he himself, Webb thought, rejoining Crombie in the foyer, would be free to interview Una Bennett. He was not looking forward to it.

12

Una was sitting in an interview room at Carrington Street Police Station, her hands folded in her lap, staring into space. There was a polystyrene mug of tea in front of her, half-empty.

WDC Denton stood up as Webb entered. He raised his eyebrows interrogatively, and she shook her head. He sat down next to her, switched on the tape, went through the preliminaries. Una hadn't moved, even to acknowledge his presence.

He leant forward slightly. 'Una, I need to know what happened.' He was hoping that use of her Christian name might reach her where a more formal approach had failed.

No response.

'Could you start by telling me why you didn't return to the office after lunch?'

'Lunch?' she repeated vaguely.

Webb said in an aside to Liz Denton, 'Has a doctor seen her?'

'Yes, Guv. She's OK to be interviewed.'

You could have fooled him. 'Are you all right, Una? Would you –?'

She moved suddenly, making him jump, and gave a choking laugh. 'Oh, I'm fine, fine. Why shouldn't I be? In the last four days, I've discovered the bodies of two members of my family. Things couldn't be better.'

Webb said quietly, 'Can you tell me what you did this afternoon?'

With a visible effort, she dragged her eyes up to his face. They were like caverns in the pallor of her face. 'I took a couple of hours off. Wonderful timing, wasn't it?'

'Did you meet Neil Crawford?'

She looked blank. 'Neil? Why should I meet him?'

'Please answer the question.'

'Of course I didn't, not until –' She broke off, clenching her hands till the bones cracked.

'So where did you go?'

'House-hunting.'

The reply was so unexpected that Webb simply stared at her. 'House-hunting?' he repeated in bewilderment.

'Yes; I intend to sell the house, and as I was passing an estate agent's, I stopped to look in the window.'

'And?' Webb prompted, when she didn't continue.

'And I spent the afternoon looking at houses. Or a cottage and a flat, to be exact.'

'Were you alone?'

She gave the ghost of a smile. 'No, I was escorted by a very enthusiastic young man. You can check.'

'What time did you get back to the town centre?'

'Quarter past three.'

'Yet you didn't arrive at the office till after four?'

'I had tea at the King's Head.'

Webb's eyebrows lifted. It seemed uncharacteristic behaviour, but at the moment he did not question it, asking again, 'Alone?'

This time she nodded, and he registered that she had no alibi for that unlikely but crucial interlude.

'I want you to tell me in detail what happened from the moment you left the King's Head.'

'I walked back along King Street. There was a police car outside Dring's. It drew up as I was passing and some uniformed men got out.'

He'd check that. 'Yes?'

'I went into Lowther Building, but there was a crowd waiting for the lift. Someone said it was stuck on the second floor.' She shuddered.

'So what did you do?'

'Used the other ones. And as I turned into our corridor I – I saw him.' She caught her lower lip in her teeth.

'Was anyone else in sight?'

'No.'

'Did you hear anything – a door shutting, or the sound of running footsteps?'

'No, nothing.'

'And you hadn't seen anyone after getting out of the lift?'

She shook her head.

'All right, go on. What exactly did you see?'

'This figure lying on the floor. I didn't know who it was, of course. Not then. I thought someone had had a heart attack. It was only when I got closer that I saw the knife. Even then I'd no idea it was Neil.'

'What did you do?' Webb asked again.

'Panicked, I suppose. Tried to pull the knife out. Then that stupid girl started to scream. I told her to dial 999, and bent down to see if he was still alive. That was when I recognized him.'

The hypothetical scenario he'd outlined to Daisy Saunders.

'Do you know what he was doing outside your offices?'

'How *could* I know? He was dead, he could hardly tell me!' Her voice had started to rise.

'You hadn't an appointment with him?'

'Of course not; if I'd wanted to see Neil – which I didn't – I'd have done so at home. My private life has no place in the office.'

'But he wanted to see you. Why else would he be in Lowther Building?'

'I tell you, I've no idea.'

'Was there any business of your husband's he might have wanted to discuss with you?'

'We'll never know, will we?'

'Nothing that you're aware of?'

'No.'

'When had you last seen him?'

'When I last saw all of them, except Jane – at the birthday party.'

So no one had been near her since. Webb felt a twinge of pity. 'Was the atmosphere at the party quite amicable?'

'Reasonably, apart from Neil. He was never amicable.' She paused, eyeing him thoughtfully. 'He more or less accused

Malcolm of squandering public funds by having lunch with you at the Grill House.'

Webb raised an eyebrow. 'It was a birthday celebration.'

'So Malcolm told us.'

'Did he tell you Mr Crawford went to see him at the station?'

Una frowned. 'No?'

'He wanted a loan, I believe.'

'Did he get it?'

'No.'

She said drily, 'You obviously know more of my family's affairs than I do, Chief Inspector.'

'I only mention it because I wondered if perhaps, now Malcolm's dead, he was going to try his luck with you.'

'He'd have had to be pretty desperate.'

'You didn't like him, did you?'

'No, and it was mutual. To be frank, I always felt I'd have had more chance of being accepted by the family without his continual sniping. However, don't run away with the idea that I killed him, because I didn't, whatever that girl said to the contrary.'

'Perhaps Mr Crawford had learned something about your husband's death, which he wanted to discuss with you?'

'Blackmail, you mean? I wouldn't put it past him, but since I didn't kill Malcolm either, it wouldn't have worked, would it? Or am I still a suspect for that, as well?'

'Everyone remains a suspect, Mrs Bennett, until someone is formally charged.'

'And I do have a habit of finding the bodies of my nearest, if not always dearest. Yes, I see your point.' She lifted her chin. '*Am* I going to be charged, then? With one or the other, or both?'

'Not at the moment.'

She seemed surprised. 'You mean I can go?'

'I'm releasing you on police bail. Which means you'll have to report back here in two months' time.'

'In other words, you're hedging your bets.'

'You could put it like that.' Webb hesitated. 'Will you be going back to Miss Wood's?'

'God, no! She's only just got rid of me, poor woman.'

'I don't think you should be alone.'

'Chief Inspector, Neil's death is a shock, but I certainly shan't be grieving for him. I'll be all right.'

'Then Miss Denton here will run you home.'

'What about my car? It's still in the office car park.'

'I think it would be unwise to drive back to Lethbridge yourself. It'll be safe enough where it is overnight.'

'Since the place is crawling with policemen, no doubt it will.'

She stood up and swayed slightly, reaching out for the table to steady herself. Meeting his eyes, she gave a rueful smile. 'Perhaps I'm not quite as tough as I thought I was.'

He rose, too. 'Good night, Mrs Bennett. Try to get some sleep.'

Actually, he saw when he glanced at his watch that it was only seven o'clock. Somehow, it felt much later. He went upstairs to find Alan Crombie back at his desk.

'Everything put to bed for the night?'

'Yep. What did Mrs Bennett have to say for herself?'

'That she'd no idea what he was doing there, and she found him on the floor with the knife in him.'

'What have you done with her?'

'Released her on police bail. I had a word with the CPS earlier, so they're aware of events so far. I'll give them an update tomorrow.'

'Bit of a coincidence, tripping over two bodies in a week – specially of her own family.'

'She admitted as much. Actually, Alan, coincidence is right. If she didn't do it – and I have a gut feeling that she didn't – I think we'll have to dismiss the idea of the job being the reason for Bennett's death. With Crawford's following on so close, it's beginning to look more like a family vendetta.'

Crombie stared at him. 'You mean the rest of them could be in danger?'

'I certainly hope not, but they should be put on their guard. I've had a bad feeling about this case from the start, and I like it even less now. We'll have to go more deeply into family backgrounds, including that of the first wife. Miss Wood can help with that.'

'Which reminds me, she left a message in case you wanted to contact her. Said she'd gone to Sally Crawford's and would be staying as long as she was needed.'

'Poor woman. She's having to cope with them all – Jane, Una and now Sally. Did she say how Sally is?'

Crombie shook his head. 'If she's feeding the baby, she probably can't even take sedatives.'

Webb let that go. Such intricacies were beyond him. 'By the way, Mrs Bennett saw a cop car in King Street this afternoon. Was there some trouble?'

'Another shop raid. What with everything else, I forgot to tell you.'

'That's all we need. Any details?'

'Three hooded youths, same as usual. They got away with the takings.'

'Um.' The raid triggered another thought. 'Was Neil Crawford robbed?'

'No, wallet intact, credit cards and everything. He was wearing an expensive watch, too.'

'So it wasn't a mugging gone wrong. But then the objects taken from the Bennett house were probably a blind, like the breaking of the glass. Robbery wasn't the motive there, either. I just wish to hell I knew what was.'

He rubbed a hand over his face. 'I suppose a press release has gone out?'

'Yes; a conference was already fixed for nine in the morning. No point in bringing it forward, is there?'

'No, it can wait till then. Did the support group have anything to report from the other offices?'

Crombie shook his head. 'Despite the reduction in lifts, no one remembers going up with Crawford. I'd say that's pretty conclusive; the office crowd tend to know each other, and they were all sure no stranger got in with them.'

'What time scale was covered?'

'Midday to four p.m.'

Webb nodded. 'And Mrs Bennett?'

'No one saw her, either.'

'She said there was a crowd when she got there, because the lift was stuck – which, if true, would mean Crawford was already dead. And if they were all staring up at the indicator, it's quite possible no one noticed her.'

He sat for a minute or two, staring broodingly down at his desk. 'Crawford's friends, acquaintances and business colleagues will have to be rounded up, to see if there's any common denominator with his father-in-law. We'll get on to that in the morning.'

'The deaths *must* be connected, surely?'

'What worries me is the difference in MO. Bennett was killed by a series of blows to the head, Crawford by a knife. It's unusual, but we have to keep an open mind.

'So, let's think: since Crawford was out and about during office hours, he presumably had an appointment. It will be interesting to know who with. In fact' – he glanced again at his watch – 'since we don't know who he worked for, and it's too late to get hold of them anyway, I'll have to ring Sally after all.'

He looked up her number in the file in front of him, and started to dial. It was a relief when Barbara Wood's voice answered.

'Chief Inspector – I was expecting to hear from you.'

'How is she, Miss Wood?'

'Numb. Going round in a trance, poor child. She can't take it in.'

'I was going to leave her till tomorrow, but there are a couple of things I need to know. Perhaps you can tell me. Do you happen to know where her husband worked?'

'Yes, with Mattison and Freebody. They're solicitors, in Silver Street.'

Webb made a note. 'Thanks. And has Sally any idea what his plans were for today?'

'He was late going into work, because someone came to see the car – he's put it up for sale. And he told Sally he had an appointment with a client later.'

'Does she know who that was?'

'I don't think so. But she also said he was going to see his bank manager this afternoon.'

'Which bank is that?'

'The National, in King Street.'

Webb had met the manager, George Latimer, who was married to a friend of Hannah's. It was highly unlikely he'd have had anything to do with the death.

'What time was the appointment?'

'I'm sorry, I don't know.'

'Never mind, there'll be a note in his office diary.'

'Is – Mrs Bennett all right?'

'Shocked, as you can imagine. She's gone home. Have you any idea why Mr Crawford should have been calling at her office?'

'None whatever. We're all totally mystified.'

Join the club, Webb thought sourly. 'All right, Miss Wood, thank you. I'll be round in the morning. Will you be there?'

'Yes. I've arranged to have tomorrow off. I – didn't take any leave earlier.'

Because, Webb thought, Una had insisted on going straight back to work, and Barbara could scarcely do less.

'I'm sure Sally'll be glad of your support,' he said. 'See you in the morning, then.'

He sat back in his chair, doodling absent-mindedly. It wasn't difficult to guess the reason for Crawford's appointment at the bank: the vexed question of a loan. That things were biting was clear from the proposed sale of the car.

Suddenly he slammed his hand down on the desk, making Crombie jump. 'I've had enough, Alan; my mind's starting to atrophy. How about a pint at the Brown Bear on the way home?'

'You're on!' Crombie closed his file with alacrity and the two men, shelving their problems till the next day, went down the stairs and out into the cold March night.

He was shuddering uncontrollably, having spent most of the last two hours vomiting over the lavatory bowl.

Why had it all gone so wrong? He'd realized almost at once that he'd dropped the ring, but Gary'd slammed the van door and Wayne started up before he could get out. Then, as they swung round the corner into Franklyn Street, he'd looked back and seen that guy pick it up.

Well, he'd done his nut, hadn't he, fighting and struggling to get out, while Gary and Kevin held on to him, not knowing what he was on about. They fell around all over the place, till Kev yelled at Wayne to stop the van and at Gary to let him go. 'Though if you're nabbed, Dean,' he'd said warningly, 'you're on your own. Remember that.'

As the van screeched to a halt, Dean grabbed Kev's knife. It would cut out arguments, and he *had* to get the ring back. If that guy took it to the police, they'd know whose it was all right.

Ignoring Kev's angry yell, he'd started to run back to the corner, rounding it in time to see his quarry turn into the building a few yards ahead of him. Quickening his pace, Dean ran after him, straight into the lift as the door was closing.

Out of breath, he leaned for a moment against the side of the lift, the knife behind him, relieved to see his companion was still holding the ring.

'That's mine,' he said between gasps. 'Can I have it back, please?' Nice and polite, like, even though the blood was thundering in his ears.

The man looked at him then, his fist closing over the ring. 'Yours?'

'Yeah, me mam gave it me,' he'd lied. 'Come on, mate, give it back.'

The guy was still looking at him with narrowed eyes, and he began to panic, expecting the lift to stop at any minute.

'Well, if it is yours, you'll have to prove it, because it looks to me very like one belonging to DCI Bennett, who was murdered last week. I hope for your sake you're telling the truth, because you're not wearing your hood now and I can give them a pretty good description of you if necessary.'

Then the lift had stopped with a jerk, and he'd started to get out. Well, he'd had to stop him, hadn't he? Couldn't let him go, when –

He lashed out blindly, and the bloke went crashing to the ground. He'd snatched the ring out of his hand and fled down the corridor, expecting at any minute to hear shouts behind him. There was a door marked 'Emergency Exit' and he'd gone clattering down the stone stairs until the flight ended near a door leading to a car park. Lungs nearly bursting, he'd flung himself outside and, ten minutes later, prosaically caught the bus home.

He hadn't *meant* to kill him, he thought now, frightened tears mingling with the sweat. It wasn't like Bennett, where everything had been planned to the last detail. But the guy had somehow recognized the ring, and seen his face into the bargain.

Suddenly Dean went cold. The gang would know it was him that done it. They wouldn't normally grass, but what if the cops traced the knife back to Kev? If the only way Kev could save himself was by shopping Dean, then he'd shop him. Stood to reason.

The clock on the mantelpiece chimed nine. He switched on the television, waiting with held breath for the news. It was about the third item: a picture of King Street – funny, seeing it on the telly – and that building he'd run into.

The announcer was saying, 'The murdered man, Neil Crawford, was the son-in-law of the detective inspector who was murdered in the nearby town of Lethbridge last Saturday, and police are considering the strong possibility of a link between the crimes.'

Bennett's *son-in-law*? Dean's eyes were starting out of his head. Of all the bloody people in the bloody world to have found the ring, it had to be the copper's son-in-law! *That's* why he'd recognized it! But why should the cops think there was a connection? They didn't know about the ring; he'd bloody killed the man so they wouldn't get it. They couldn't link it to him without it – could they?

Slowly he bent forward until his forehead was resting on his knees and began, despairingly, to weep.

13

After the press conference the next morning, Webb rang through to Lethbridge to let them know he'd be spending the day in Shillingham on the Crawford case. Jeff Carter asked to speak to him, and was put on the line.

'You know I was going to the Oliver Cromwell last night, sir, to track down Kevin Baker?'

'Yes?'

'I'm sorry to say there was no sign of him. Might be lying low after the latest raid – always supposing he was involved. Still, we'll keep looking.'

'Did you have a word with Don about Clark and Cooch?'

'Yes; so far, they've not admitted to knowing anything about the raids or anyone called Kevin. But DS Partridge says Clark's showing signs of strain; he's still hoping to get something useful out of him.' He paused. 'Too bad about Mr Crawford.'

Webb smiled wryly. 'Your prime suspect gone for a burton, Jeff! Any other ideas?'

'I still think it's family rather than job based.'

'After this one, I'm coming round to agreeing with you. It mightn't be a bad idea to keep a discreet eye on the house; Mrs Bennett will be there alone at night, and we don't want any more fatalities.'

'Right, sir. I'll be in touch if anything else comes up this end. And we'll give the pub another try tonight.'

'All in the line of duty?'

'Of course, sir.'

Webb put down the phone with a grin, which faded as he

dialled the National Bank and asked to be put through to the manager.

'Mr Latimer? DCI Webb; I think we have met.'

Latimer murmured some reply.

'You know why I'm phoning, of course. It seems you're in the unfortunate position of being the last person to see Mr Crawford.'

'It's quite appalling, Chief Inspector – I can't believe it.'

'Could you tell me the nature of the interview he had with you?'

Latimer hesitated. 'Do I assume confidentiality is waived in a murder case?'

'You do indeed, sir.'

'Then I must tell you he was in financial difficulties. He requested a loan, which I wasn't able to agree to.'

'What frame of mind was he in when he left you?'

'Disappointed, bitter, even a little desperate, perhaps.'

'Did he mention going on anywhere? To see his step-mother, for instance?'

'No; in fact, I had the impression that he'd as little as possible to do with his in-laws.'

'What time was his appointment?'

'Three-thirty.'

'And he left when?'

'About fifteen minutes later.'

Webb thanked him, told him someone would call to take a formal statement, and put down the phone.

'Exactly what time was that raid at the supermarket?' he asked Crombie.

The inspector flicked through some papers. 'The call was logged at fifteen-fifty.'

'That's what I thought; Crawford would just have left the bank, and it's only a few doors from the supermarket. He'd have been right on the spot. Suppose he recognized one of the gang?'

'Seems unlikely,' Crombie said, unimpressed. 'For one thing they were wearing balaclavas, and for another they'd hardly move in the same circles, would they? Even if he *did* recognize someone, it wouldn't have been worth killing him for.'

Webb grunted. 'What time did the squad car get there?'

Crombie's finger ran down the report. 'Just after sixteen hundred.'

'Una Bennett says she saw it arrive, which, if true, means that by walking at a normal pace she'd have reached Lowther Building at about five past four and the second floor shortly after. You know, Alan, in view of the fact that the lift was already jammed – which was confirmed by the support group – I honestly don't see how she could have done it.'

'No, I agree it would be too easy. Not many killers are obliging enough to hang round waiting to be discovered with the weapon in their hands.'

'If we agree it's a family thing, who else have we got?'

'Well, it's unlikely to be an actual member. Probably just someone that hates the lot of them.'

'Why?'

'You tell me.'

Webb sighed and stood up. 'All this idle conjecture is simply to delay going to see Sally. But it's no good, I can't put it off any longer.'

'Is there such a thing as bereavement fatigue?'

'If there is,' Webb said over his shoulder as he left the room, 'that poor girl is a prime candidate.'

When Webb and Jackson reached Chedbury, however, it was to be told by a drawn-looking Barbara Wood that Sally was sleeping.

'I'll wake her, of course, if it's necessary, but she hardly slept last night and she does need some rest. The trouble is, the baby senses something's wrong, and has been playing up. I've only just got him settled.'

She glanced out of the window at the pram in the garden.

Webb's eyes fell to the newspaper on the coffee table, with its lurid black headlines: **MURDERED POLICEMAN'S SON-IN-LAW FOUND SLAIN**.

Following his gaze, Barbara said quietly, 'I hid it from Sally, but when she went upstairs I took it out to see if there was anything new.'

'Not so far,' Webb told her.

'Do you think it was the same person who killed Malcolm?'

'It would be an odd coincidence if it weren't, and I tend not to believe in coincidences.' He hesitated. 'It's just possible someone has a grudge against the whole family. Without wanting to be alarmist, it wouldn't hurt to take extra care for the moment. See that no one goes out alone, and so on.'

She regarded him with horror. 'You mean we might all be targeted?'

'It's only a possibility, but better safe than sorry. In the circumstances, we're having to delve even further into family history, which, of course, includes yours and your late sister's. Are there any members of your own family who might have resented Mr Bennett marrying again, for instance?'

'Certainly not. We were all happy for him.'

'I'm sure you speak for yourself, but others might not have been so understanding.'

'But Carol died, Chief Inspector. It's not as though he left her for someone else.' She paused. 'Surely it's more likely to have stemmed from Malcolm's job?'

'After this second killing, we're not so sure.'

'He sometimes discussed his cases with me, and I've been torturing myself, wondering whether I could have prevented his death.'

'I'm quite sure you couldn't.' Webb looked at her reflectively. 'What cases did he mention lately?'

'Well, there were the shop raids, of course, especially the one when the assistant was injured. He was afraid someone might be killed if they went on much longer. Then, going back a few weeks, there was that man who hanged himself in his cell – Lennie someone. Malcolm was quite upset about that.'

'Unfortunately such things happen.'

'The man was claustrophobic, he said, so prison was worse for him than for most people.'

'We're not inhuman, Miss Wood,' Webb commented. 'Arrangements would have been made –'

'Yes, but even if he was given more space, there was still the prospect of being locked up for several years. Malcolm said that's what got to him.'

'The facile answer is that he should have thought of that before. He knew the risks he was taking.'

There was a sound behind them, and they turned to see Sally in the doorway. She was wearing an old towelling robe, her hair was tousled and her swollen eyes gummed with sleep.

Webb and Jackson got to their feet. Webb said quietly, 'There's very little we can say, Sally.'

She nodded. 'Who was it? The same person who killed Dad?'

'Very probably.'

Her mouth trembled. 'I'd like to get my hands on him.'

'Is there anything you can tell us that might help? Anyone your husband had had a row with, or who held a grudge against him?'

'I don't know.' She came into the room and perched on the arm of her aunt's chair. It was the one, Webb remembered, in which Crawford had sat during their last visit. Barbara's arm went round her protectively.

'He liked to stir things up,' Sally was continuing, 'but there was never anything serious.'

Just hints of public funds being misappropriated for Malcolm to give him lunch, Webb thought.

'Why was he at Una's place, anyway?' she demanded. 'He *never* went there! When I heard where he was found, I thought she must have done it.'

'Have you remembered the name of the client he was seeing that morning?'

'It's not a question of remembering – he never mentioned it.'

'There was also someone who came to look at the car; who was that, do you know?'

'Neil just said "the friend of a friend". He – wasn't being very communicative, you see. Things had been a bit strained; he'd tried to borrow money off Dad, and I was furious. The terrible thing is we didn't have time to make it up.'

She put her hands to her face and began to cry. Webb remembered dispassionately that Crawford hadn't had an alibi for the time his father-in-law was killed. It was still possible he himself had been responsible; if so, had someone found out and avenged Malcolm? The permutations were endless.

'About the family,' he began diffidently. 'Is it a large one?'

It was Barbara who replied. 'Not really. As far as I know, Malcolm had only one sister, who lives in America.'

'Married?'

'Yes, I think there are four children. All grown up now, of course.'

'We'll need their names and addresses.' And a lot of good that would do; still, it was a means of elimination if nothing else. He waited while Jackson jotted them down.

'And on your side?'

'There was only Carol and me. We have a few cousins, but we were never close. I doubt if they either know or care that Malcolm married again.'

'I'm not saying that was the reason for his death, Miss Wood. I was only trying to think of some family-based motive.'

Sally looked up, wiping her eyes. 'You think it's to do with the *family*?'

'We were just saying that with Neil's death coming so soon after, it's possible. In view of which, it would be as well not to go out alone for the moment.'

She stared at him speechlessly, and he hurried on: 'I believe your husband worked with Mattison and Freebody in Silver Street?'

'That's right.' Her eyes dropped.

'Did he get on well with his colleagues?'

'On a business level, I think, but he wasn't specially friendly with any of them.'

'Was he happy there?'

'Not really; he was always wanting something better.'

'I know about the financial problems,' Webb said gently, 'if that makes it easier to talk.'

She said quickly, 'He didn't mean to do anything wrong,

you know. Everything would have been all right if the market hadn't dropped.'

Which was something he *didn't* know about. 'Leaving him high and dry?' he prompted.

'Before he could replace the funds, yes. He was going to – and if things had gone as he'd expected, he'd have made thousands of pounds. He only borrowed the money – you must understand that.'

So Crawford had been in deeper than he'd suspected. No wonder he'd urgently needed to get his hands on some money. But anything he'd hoped, via Sally, to gain from Malcolm's death wouldn't have come through in time to help him out of this predicament; which lessened the likelihood of his having killed him.

'What about other contacts? At the golf club, for instance?'

'He only joined because he thought it might be useful,' Sally said sadly. 'He'd no friends there.'

'What about enemies?'

She looked startled. 'Oh, I don't think so. Nothing as strong as that.'

Webb stood up. 'Thank you, Sally. I'm sorry to have to ask these things, but we need to have as clear a picture as possible.'

She nodded, her eyes full of tears again. 'Basically, you know, he was just insecure. He thought if he had a lot of money and was successful, people would like him.'

Webb nodded and awkwardly patted her arm. 'I know. Now, remember what I said about not going out alone. You're probably not in any danger, but we don't want to take chances.'

'I'll see you out,' Barbara said. At the door, she asked in a low voice, 'Should I arrange to stay with her indefinitely?'

'I trust it won't be "indefinitely", Miss Wood. Just about the entire force is working on Malcolm's death, and the inquiry will now expand to include Neil's. We should collar our man soon. For the moment, though, I'm sure your presence is a comfort to Sally, quite apart from adding to her safety.'

*　　　*　　　*

166

'Where now, Guv?'

'The solicitors, I think. Parking's tight in Silver Street, so when we get back to Shillingham, we'll dump the car at the station and walk round.'

Silver Street was the small road that connected the two busier thoroughfares of Franklyn Road and Duke Street. Its buildings were mainly offices, in particular those of building societies, accountants and solicitors. There was also a coffee shop, which vied for the inhabitants' custom with the Red Lion pub on the corner. The smell of baking wafted out enticingly as they passed and Jackson's footsteps flagged.

'Not now, Ken,' Webb said. 'Perhaps when we come out.'

This was a more recently established firm than many which Webb visited in the course of his duties, with modern furnishings and a less forbidding atmosphere. Chester Freebody, the senior partner, was a tall, lanky man in his forties, with bony wrists protruding from his cuffs and a prominent Adam's apple.

'This is all very distressing,' he commented, as Webb and Jackson were shown into his private office. 'Angie, bring some coffee, would you?'

'How long had Neil Crawford been working for you, Mr Freebody?'

'Four years now. We had high hopes of him.' His voice tailed off, as though he'd intended to add more, then thought better of it.

'Was he popular among the staff?'

Freebody paused, then said, 'Oh, dear! I don't like to speak ill of the dead, but since you ask, Chief Inspector, no, he wasn't. An eye to the main chance, if you know what I mean. It doesn't go down well.'

There was a tap on the door and a girl came in with three cups of coffee. Webb waited until she left before asking, 'Was there open hostility towards him?'

'Not really, just the odd dark mutters.'

'He spent some time out of the office yesterday, I believe, both in the morning and afternoon?'

'I couldn't say; I'll get his secretary.'

167

A subdued young woman, summoned by the intercom, came into the room with a desk diary.

'Can you tell us, Linda, what Neil's movements were yesterday?'

She glanced down at it. 'He'd an appointment with Mrs Berryman in Hatherley at ten o'clock, and he said it wasn't worth coming in before that.' Trying to sell his car, Webb remembered.

'I suppose it was about eleven when he got in, and he went to lunch at one.'

'Any clients call during the morning?'

'No, sir.'

'Did he meet anyone for lunch?'

'Not according to the diary.'

'Do personal appointments go in it?'

'If they're during working hours. It does say, "Bank: 3.30".'

'This Mrs Berryman; what would he be seeing her about?'

'Oh, nothing spectacular,' Freebody put in. 'She wanted to make a new will. She could quite easily have come here, but she's a wealthy client and likes us to dance attendance.'

Webb turned back to the secretary. 'And after lunch?'

'He came back about two-thirty and went out again at three-fifteen, to the bank.' She bit her lip. 'That was the last time I saw him.'

'Thanks, Linda.' Freebody nodded to her, and she left the room. Webb's mobile phone shrilled in his pocket. He excused himself and moved to a corner.

'Spider?' demanded a voice, before he could speak.

The Chief Super, checking up on progress. 'Yes, sir.'

'Wonder if you could look in at Stonebridge later this morning? I'd like a word.'

'Of course, sir.'

'Where are you at the moment?'

'At the solicitors' where Crawford worked.'

'Right. See you in an hour or so.'

Webb returned to his chair. 'Sorry about that.' He turned back to Freebody. 'Was there anyone Mr Crawford was particularly at odds with? Who might have resented him more than most?'

Freebody raised his eyebrows. 'Are you asking if a member of my staff is a potential murderer?'

Webb smiled ruefully. 'I suppose I am.'

'Then I'm glad to say, no, there wasn't. I keep an eye open for anything of that nature; in a small office, petty animosities can quickly blow up if they're not stamped out.'

With which, for the moment, Webb had to be content. 'Thanks for your help, Mr Freebody. We shall be interviewing your staff later; Crawford might have mentioned something useful.' Such as the identity of the potential car-buyer, though, on reflection, that was unlikely. He wouldn't have admitted to his colleagues that he was selling it.

'It was the Chief Super on the blower,' he told Jackson as they walked back to Carrington Street. 'He wants me to call in, a.s.a.p. No point in dragging you out to Stonebridge; you can use the time getting your paperwork up to date and I'll meet you back here at two.'

Constabulary Headquarters was situated in the middle of the Broadshire countryside. There was no village within miles, and it took its name from the stone bridge that crossed the Avon and Broadshire Canal some yards farther down the road. Webb drove round the corner to the car park and went inside.

Chief Superintendent Phil Fleming was fresh-faced, bright-eyed and highly intelligent. Webb liked him, though he wished he would drop that irritating nickname, invented by an old lag years before. It was still in circulation, but no one else dared use it to his face.

'Now, Spider,' Fleming began before he was properly into the room, 'fill me in on how things are going.'

'Well, we are making progress, sir. Reports are coming in all the time and being checked against each other. I don't need to tell you everyone's working flat out on this one.'

Fleming nodded gravely. 'This latest death – the son-in-law. Any connection?'

'I think there has to be. The murder weapon's at the lab going through tests at the moment. If there are any finger-prints other than Mrs Bennett's, we're in with a chance.'

'Different MO though, isn't it? How do you account for that?'

'At the moment I can't, sir,' Webb said frankly.

'If he was in the habit of carrying a knife, why not use it on Bennett instead of lugging in a piece of wood?'

'That's the big question. It seems likely, by the way, that he was waiting in the house for Bennett to come home.'

Fleming cocked his head, his bird-bright eyes on Webb's face. 'How do you make that out?'

'Mrs Bennett had the impression someone was there when she returned briefly just beforehand.'

'In the clear herself, would you say?'

'Well, sir, she found both bodies, and we know how many killers claim to do that. It's still possible she murdered her husband, though I think we can rule her out on Crawford. The devil of it is, the timing's very tight in both cases and she's been within a hair's breadth each time.'

'Prefer it not to be her,' Fleming said gruffly. 'Anyone else in the frame?'

'Not as yet. We're concentrating on two fronts now, family and work. We're sure to come up with something soon.'

He sounded more confident than he felt. But damn it, they *had* to, and not, in this instance, because top brass were restive and the press baying for blood as usual. This time it was because one of their own had been murdered, a man who had lived and laughed and cursed among them for many years, who had shared the same dangers, frustrations and sheer bloody hard work as the rest of them; a man, furthermore, who had believed in a decent, law-abiding society and who, in the end, had given his life trying to achieve it. Because, for all his reservations, Webb still felt they'd find the reason for Malcolm's death buried in his case files. Though how the hell Crawford's tied in with it was another matter entirely.

14

Late that afternoon there was a double breakthrough; a message came from the lab to say the knife which killed Crawford was the same as that which had stabbed Michelle Taylor in the Lethbridge off-licence. There was a nick out of the blade, matching both wounds. Furthermore, a footprint taken from the lift in Lowther Building was identical with one from the newsagent's in Dick Lane, thus tying two of the raids firmly in with the murder.

With fingerprints, they were less fortunate; only Mrs Bennett's had shown up clearly. Two other smudged sets were not distinct enough to check against records.

The fact that it was Crawford's death rather than Bennett's that tied in with the raids was puzzling. Had he died simply because he'd come out of the bank while a raid was in progress, or was there more to it? And if he *was* killed because he saw something, why not there and then, on the pavement, instead of outside Una Bennett's office?

Come to that, they were no nearer knowing why Crawford had gone there, particularly if someone was after him.

As to the killer, it must surely be 'Kev', who had used the knife in the Lethbridge raid. It was imperative that they find him as soon as possible, but so far their leads were minimal; only the name itself, a different getaway vehicle each time, and the fact that there seemed to be four in the gang. It wasn't much to go on, and the manager in King Street had been unable to add to it.

The change of vans might be significant; possibly one of them worked at a second-hand dealer's. He'd get Bob Dawson on to that. Then there were Clark and Cooch, small-time crooks who might well mix with others – and Partridge had thought they might cough. He lifted the phone.

'Don, those two lads you interviewed; have another go at them, will you, on the shop-raid gang? We're looking at murder now; the knife which killed Crawford is the one used in the Lethbridge raid. And there's something else: they've always gone for the smaller shops before. This time, they're confident enough to tackle a supermarket. Is it just coincidence that Clark and Cooch both work in one, or could they have passed on tips? It's a long shot, but worth a try. Oh, and get John Manning to dig out all we've got on any Kevins who've come our way, particularly the Kevin Baker DS Carter mentioned. He's moved from the address they have on file, but dammit, he must live somewhere. Try the DSS.'

Webb sat back in his seat, staring moodily across the room. It was barely five days since Malcolm's death, but already he was feeling the need to set what he knew down on paper, an urge which usually came later in a case. He'd a niggling suspicion that there were connections which he hadn't made and which were there for the searching.

His habit of 'drawing conclusions' was well known in the force, and had often opened up previously unsuspected avenues leading to the villain.

He looked at his watch. Five-thirty. 'I'm knocking off early this evening, Alan; I want to sort a few things out in my mind. If anything important comes up, give me a buzz at home.'

In each case it was the motive that was so baffling, he thought as he drove through the rush-hour traffic. Find the motive, and they'd find the killer – only one, he was convinced, for both murders. But what had Malcolm and Neil in common, other than their relationship? And how could that concern a gang of thieves?

He turned up the hill out of town, past the entrance to Montpellier Gardens where Hannah's school was. She'd be home by now. He wondered if, despite his reassurances, she was still uneasy about Susan's reappearance.

Having let himself into the flat and poured a stiff drink, he went to the phone and dialled her number.

'I've been reading about the latest murder,' she said, after they'd exchanged banalities. 'There's a photo of the victim in the *News*, and it says he's your friend's son-in-law.'

'That's right.'

'But how awful, David. Does it mean the same person killed him?'

'That, my love, is what we have to discover. Not to mention his identity. Which leads me to the point of this phone call; have you anything on this evening?'

'No, why?'

'Could I stick my neck out and invite myself to supper? A lateish one, though. I've got the bit between my teeth – or rather, a pencil between my fingers – and I want to spend some time getting things down. But I'd also like to see you, and this seemed a good, if selfish, way of achieving both ends.'

'You're doing your drawing already? Isn't it rather early?'

'Yes, but we can't hang around on this one. None of us can settle to anything while this brute's on the loose, and the sooner we nab him, the happier everyone will be.'

'Fair enough. And of course you're welcome to supper. Eight o'clock? Nine?'

'Let's split the difference and say eight-thirty. Bless you, Hannah.'

He set up his easel in the living-room, pulled over a stool and a table for his drink and crayons, and settled down. He'd do the two crimes separately first, before checking for common features. The background, then: the Bennett sitting-room, and, across the hall, the kitchen with its broken pane of glass.

His pencil moved rapidly over the paper, marking out the layout of the ground floor. Then he drew a stick figure representing Malcolm in his easy chair. Normally, when he knew the people involved, he fleshed them out as easily recognizable caricatures, but he couldn't bring himself to subject Malcolm to this treatment.

There *could* have been a shadowy figure in the background, that presence which Una had felt, and which might or might not have been imaginary. However, under his self-imposed rules, no hypotheses were allowed in this exercise and only known facts could be included.

So, assuming the time of death to be roughly one-thirty, where exactly had the suspects been? Come to that, *who* were they? Una, certainly, who in the first instance hadn't admitted returning to the house. According to her statement, she'd have been on her way to Steeple Bayliss. He sketched in a car at the far edge of the paper.

Neil Crawford was another; allegedly he'd been at the DIY centre at the time, but he had no alibi. Though Webb strongly believed him to be a victim of the same killer, there was still no proof of this, so he must make his appearance. In another corner, a few strokes of the pencil produced a startlingly life-like figure beside a notice reading 'DIY'.

Steven Clark also had no alibi; what was more, he'd a grudge – albeit a small one – against Malcolm, and, as they'd now discovered, criminal tendencies. In a third corner, his form took shape, seated before a television set.

And lastly there was the unknown Kevin, whom Webb, breaking all his rules, uncompromisingly placed behind Malcolm's chair. He was, after all, the most likely bet.

One by one he studied his cast of suspects, each distinguished by a different colour: black for Una's hair and eyes, yellow for the blond Crawford, brown for Clark's jacket, and green for Kevin's balaclava – if it *was* Kevin. And that was about it. Not a very promising start. Before abandoning the drawing, he sketched Malcolm's missing ring in the final corner, which completed just about all they had on the case.

He let the paper fall to the floor and took another sheet, this time sketching King Street, with the hotel on the corner of Gloucester Circus, and, across the road, the National Bank, Dring's Superstore and Lowther Building, all of which had featured in the case. Then he sat staring at it for a long time.

Exactly what had happened in those ten crucial minutes? Una had walked back from the King's Head, Neil had left the bank, the supermarket had been raided. Were those facts connected, and if so, how?

He reproduced the figures from the first sheet, putting them in appropriate positions: Neil outside the bank, the helmeted figure by the store, Una by the King's Head – since by the time she reached the supermarket, the police had arrived.

The knife tied one of the raiders in with the murder; but why kill Neil, an innocent bystander? Previously those injured had been staff of the targeted shop. Had he tried to prevent their getaway? But if so, he'd surely have been stabbed in front of the store? Above all, why did one of the perpetrators waste precious time going after him instead of making his escape? None of it made sense.

Almost without thinking, Webb tore off a third sheet and depicted the scene on the second floor: the open lift, the sprawled body with Una Bennett bending over it, and Daisy Saunders with her wide, screaming mouth.

SOCO had reported shoe prints in the lift and leading along the corridor to the emergency exit. Another had been lifted from a stone step halfway down, then the trail went cold. Had the getaway van waited at a prearranged spot, or had there been no time to arrange a rendezvous?

Webb made a note to check that all shops and offices in King Street and Franklyn Street had been contacted, and everyone asked if they'd seen anyone running from the scene.

He went to the kitchen to refresh his drink, then took up his position again. The clock ticked slowly on as he sat there, staring first at one drawing, then another. There was something he was missing, he was sure of it. But what? Perhaps after all it was too early in the case to embark on this exercise.

When he finally abandoned it, it was after eight and he'd only time for a quick wash before going downstairs to join Hannah.

'Any luck?' she greeted him.

He shook his head dispiritedly.

'Barbara Wood phoned me to request leave, for at least the rest of this week. I believe she's with her niece?'

'Yes; the poor girl's in a bad way. Hardly surprising, when her father and husband have been murdered within four days of each other.'

Hannah shuddered. 'And you still don't know why?'

'At this moment, love, I haven't a clue. That's what bugs me.'

'You need some food inside you,' she said practically. 'That will help to put things in perspective.'

'You're right; I had to go over to Stonebridge at lunchtime, so I only managed a sandwich.'

Hannah chatted lightly during the meal, but for the most part Webb was too tired to make the effort to reply. The emotional undertone of this case was taking it out of all of them, everyone slogging his guts out to avenge Malcolm, and the strain was beginning to tell.

During coffee, he put his hand over Hannah's. 'Sorry to be such poor company, love, but that was just what I needed. Your company as much as the meal.'

'Would you like to stay?'

'Better not; as you'll have gathered, I'm in need of an early night and there's another long day tomorrow.'

She noted his drawn face and the circles under his eyes. She, too, would be glad when this case was over, for Barbara's sake as well as David's. His work didn't usually touch her so closely and she could only be grateful. At least it seemed that Susan's coming had passed without repercussions, though she hadn't dared raise the subject.

At the door, he stood holding her tightly for several minutes. Then he kissed her good night, and she closed the door after him.

Back in his own flat, Webb showered and prepared for bed, his mind returning again and again to the papers on his abandoned easel. Forget it, he told himself firmly, or you'll be no good for anything tomorrow.

He was about to get into bed when the phone rang. With a frown, he glanced at the clock, surprised to see it was only ten-thirty.

'Webb.'

It was the duty sergeant at Carrington Street. 'Sorry to disturb you, sir, but we've got the manager of Dring's Superstore on the line – name of Stamp.'

Webb's tiredness melted away. 'Yes?'

'He wants to speak to the officer in charge of the Crawford case – insists it's urgent. All right if I say you'll ring him back? He won't speak to anyone else.'

'Certainly, Sergeant, let me have his number.'

He scribbled it down on a pad and promptly dialled it. A nervous voice answered at once. 'Bernard Stamp.'

Webb sat down on the bed. 'This is Chief Inspector Webb, Mr Stamp. I believe you want to speak to me.'

'Oh yes, Chief Inspector. I'm sorry it's so late but I've been out and only just seen the evening paper. That man who was killed – Neil Crawford –'

'Yes?'

'I recognized him at once. He was outside the store when the raiders ran out.'

Webb's hand tightened on the phone. 'Yes?' he said again.

'Well, he told me the van had turned down Franklyn Street, but it was only when I saw his picture that I realized he was the one who'd been killed. And I've remembered something else he said: he told me one of them had dropped something.'

Webb rose slowly to his feet. 'Go on.'

'Well, I'm awfully sorry, I wasn't really paying attention. All I could think of was that we'd lost the day's takings, and then I saw a policeman across the road and was desperate to attract his attention. He ran over and I told him what had happened, and when I next looked round, the other chap had gone.'

'Did he say *what* the thief had dropped?'

'No, but it must have been small, because he was holding it in his hand.'

'What were his exact words, do you remember?'

'I've been trying to. I think he said – "They went round the corner. I didn't get their number, but one of them dropped this." But I – I'm afraid I didn't look to see what it was. Could it be important?'

Webb closed his eyes on a wave of exasperation. 'Yes, Mr Stamp, it could very well be vital. Have you no idea at all?'

'Absolutely none, I'm afraid. I'm sorry.'

'Never mind, what you've told me is a great help. Thank you for calling.'

Webb walked back into the living-room and stood in front of the easel, excitement moving inside him. Neil had picked up something the thieves had dropped. That, it seemed crystal-clear, was why he died. But what could he have found that was so incriminating it was worth killing for? Would it identify the thief in some way? Or tie him in with something much more serious than raiding shops?

His eyes moved slowly over the sheets he'd worked on earlier. And suddenly there it was, its yellow crayon seeming to shine like real gold in an effort to attract his attention. Malcolm's ring!

A wave of heat sluiced over him. Could it have been? Suppose one of the raiders – the killer – had been wearing it, and in the panic of running out of the shop had somehow dropped it and Neil picked it up? It *had* to be that, because here at last was the only possible explanation for Neil's going to Una's office. *He'd wanted her to identify it.*

It also explained the time-lapse in his death; his killer must have seen him pick it up, and run back to retrieve it. He hadn't bothered to rob Neil; all he'd wanted was the incriminating ring.

So now they had a motive for Neil's murder, if not Malcolm's. The killings were connected, as they'd always thought, but only because Neil had stumbled on the ring; he'd not been an intended victim. The question now was why a petty criminal who stole from shops should have gone so far out of his league as to murder a policeman.

But that would have to wait till morning. The central heating had gone off and he was starting to shiver, as much from tiredness as the cold. His mind buzzing with new possibilities, Webb went to bed.

At Carrington Street the next morning, he lost no time in bringing the team up to date. As he'd supposed, shops and offices in the area had been questioned, but nothing positive had emerged. The occupants had been at their desks or behind their counters, and hadn't noticed what was happening outside in the street. An appeal to the general public would go out after the regional news that evening.

Having briefed his action teams, Webb collected Jackson. 'I want to go back to Lethbridge, Ken, and see how they're faring on Kevin Baker. It looks as though he's the one we're after. He's had a couple of convictions for burglary, but when

I spoke to Jeff we didn't know he was implicated in the DCI's death. I want to know if Mr Bennett had any personal dealings with him.'

'We've not got anywhere, sir,' Carter reported, frustration in his voice. 'He's disappeared off the face of the earth, and Gary Higgs with him. I've got all the snouts out looking, but no result so far.'

'It was his knife that killed Crawford, Jeff, that much has been established. And though I can't prove it yet, I'm pretty sure he was killed because Baker dropped Mr Bennett's ring. You see where that leaves us.'

Carter stared at him. 'You mean Kevin Baker murdered the governor? But he's only a petty crook, sir. He's never done anything remotely like that before.'

'That's what I wanted to speak to you about. Those convictions of his; did the DCI deal with them personally?'

'No, it was DI Stratton both times. And he only went down for a few months; it was no big deal.'

'Then could Mr Bennett have seen more than he realized at the Lethbridge off-licence? Something that could have linked Baker with it?'

'Even if he did, it wouldn't have been worth *killing* him. OK, so the stabbing was more serious than what Baker's done before, but the girl recovered.'

'Well, whatever his motive, it looks as though he's scarpered now, and Higgs with him. If we're having no luck round here, we'll have to spread our nets. Circulate their descriptions to all police stations. Any leads on the other two in the gang?'

'Not so far. The barman at the Oliver Cromwell was very cagey; afraid of frightening off his clientele by hobnobbing with the police. All we can hope –'

There was a knock on the door and Polsom, one of the older detective constables, put his head round it.

'Could I have a word, Guv?'

'Of course, come in.'

'Well, it's like this: Mr Bennett's desk has been cleared, and there were one or two personal items in it. The DI asked me to take them round to his home.'

'Yes?'

'Well, sir, the cleaner opened the door, and you could have knocked me down with a feather. Know who it was?'

He waited expectantly and Webb said testily, 'We're not here to play guessing games, Polsom.'

'No, sir, sorry, sir. Well, it was Rita Jones, Lennie's widow. How about that?'

'Lennie – ?' The name seemed faintly familiar.

'The bloke who topped himself in jail,' Carter said, his voice beginning to rise with excitement. 'That's a bit rum, wouldn't you say, sir?'

A widow with a son on the dole, repeated Una's voice in his head. Webb pushed back his chair. 'Where's the file on this Lennie Jones?'

'Here, Guv; I thought you'd want a gander at it.' Polsom, looking pleased with himself, placed the bulky package he'd been holding on the desk in front of Webb, who rapidly riffled through the pages.

It appeared that although Jones had over the years come under suspicion on several counts, such as receiving stolen goods, burglary and conspiring to defraud, he'd always managed to escape with at most a fine. Until the last time, when his misdemeanours had finally caught up with him. Bennett had been the arresting officer, and a hand-written postscript was stapled to the final sheet: *Jones claustrophobic; special arrangements necessary if custodial sentence. MB.*

Malcolm had done his best for him, Webb reflected bitterly, and, so Barbara Wood had told him, been upset at his suicide. Nevertheless, it was beginning to look as though he'd paid for it with his own life.

Webb looked up. 'But I don't understand. Surely if this woman was planning to kill Mr Bennett, she wouldn't have turned up at his house, as bold as brass? If Polsom recognized her, why the hell didn't he – or you, Jeff, for that matter, when you interviewed her?'

'Me and the governor never met her,' Carter told him. 'She

180

was in hospital when we were dealing with Lennie. Women's trouble, he said.'

'It's some time since I saw her myself, sir,' Polsom put in. 'Going on a couple of years now. She was there when DI Stratton and me collared him. Suspicion of burglary, but he wriggled out of it as per usual.'

'Even so, for her to turn up afterwards, when the SOCOs were there – it was the hell of a risk.'

'I reckon Dick here and the DI were the only two who knew her. She probably reckoned she was safe enough. And I dare say,' Carter added shrewdly, 'it gave her a buzz, tempting fate like that. A bit of excitement, like her old man's escapades gave him.'

'Good God,' Webb said numbly. 'And what about the son? Suppose he's been looking for a buzz, too?'

They all looked blank, and a quick check established that the younger Jones had no criminal record.

'Would he have known Baker and Higgs?' Webb asked Carter, who gave a low whistle.

'Highly likely, I'd say; they're all local lads. Probably at school together.'

Webb turned to Polsom. 'Did you let Mrs Jones see you recognized her?'

The man looked startled. 'Well, I –'

'*Did you, man?*'

From being complacent at the stir he'd caused, Polsom now looked abashed. 'Well, it was a surprise to see her there, Guv. It was only later –'

'So what did you say?'

'Just, "Hello, Rita, what are you doing here?"'

'And how did she react?'

'She looked taken aback, like. Muttered something about helping out, and I handed over Mr Bennett's things.'

'That was all?'

'Yessir.'

'How long ago was that?'

The constable looked at his watch. 'Half an hour or so.'

'Right, we'll get over there on the double.'

'Beg pardon, sir' – Polsom again – 'she won't be there now.

181

She was on her way out when I got there – I reckon she works nine to eleven.'

It was eleven-thirty-five. Webb glanced frustratedly at the open file. 'Then we'll call at her house. Fifty-two, Dickens Close. And we'd better make it fast – she might have taken fright.'

'What about Kevin Baker, sir?' Carter asked as they piled in the car. 'It was his knife, after all.'

'He might still be the one, Jeff. This is a new lead, that's all.' But it was more than that; he could feel it in his bones.

Dickens Close was on a small council estate to the south of the town. As the car drew up outside number 52, Webb caught a glimpse of a frightened face at an upstairs window before it darted back out of sight.

They started up the path, and Jackson suddenly shouted, 'Look out – someone's just cleared the back fence!'

He and DC Frear went hurtling round the side of the house, joined by men from the second police car which had drawn up with a screeching of brakes. Carter hammered on the front door. There was no reply. Webb lifted the flap of the letterbox and bent down to it.

'Open the door, Mrs Jones. It's the police, and we're not going away.'

After a couple of minutes there was the sound of a key turning and a bolt being drawn back and the door slowly opened to reveal a small, pointed-faced woman with frizzy hair and glasses.

He held up his warrant card. 'Rita Jones?'

She nodded, her mouth working nervously.

'May we come inside?' Webb moved into the house without waiting for an answer, Carter at his heels. Mrs Jones asserted herself.

'I don't know what you think you're doing!' she declared, folding her arms belligerently. 'Ought to be ashamed of yourselves, hassling me like this! First you kill my old man, then you come bursting in – '

'Your old man killed himself,' Webb said, glancing round

182

the shabby room in which he found himself. 'Despite Mr Bennett's efforts on his behalf.'

Fear came and went behind the glasses. 'I'm sure I don't know what you mean by that. It was Mr Bennett that done for him.'

'As you very well know, Mrs Jones, he made arrangements for Lennie to be housed in the hospital area rather than a normal cell.'

'Still locked up, though, wasn't he? Did his nut, but would they listen? No, they wouldn't!'

'So you planned revenge. You and your son.'

'Dean?' She looked alarmed. 'Nothing to do with Dean.'

On cue, some heavy knocks sounded again on the front door. At a nod from Webb, Carter went to answer it and there was the sound of voices in the hall. Then Jackson, Frear and Polsom appeared with a youth between them. His jacket was muddy, his cheek bruised and he was limping.

His mother said shrilly, 'What you done to him?'

'He fell when he was legging it down the road, Guv.' It was to Webb that Jackson spoke.

Webb regarded the surly but frightened face in front of him. There was no saying if he'd have the ring on him, but –

'Would you turn out your pockets, please?' he said, noting the surprise of his fellow officers; this was usually left until arrival at the cells, but, watching Jones, he saw the sick resignation in his eyes.

The boy hesitated for a moment. Then he slid a hand into the inner pocket of his jacket, withdrew a gold ring with a speckled green stone, and dropped it on the table. A bloodstone indeed, Webb thought sombrely; snatched from Malcolm's body and the direct cause of Crawford's death.

'What you got there?' Rita Jones exclaimed, her eyes uncomprehendingly on the ring. Webb ignored her.

'Dean Jones, I'm arresting you in connection with the murders of DCI Malcolm Bennett and Neil Crawford. You don't have to –'

'Neil who?' Rita again, her voice shrill. 'What you talking

about? Dean don't know nothing about that – let him go!'

Webb said expressionlessly, 'I'm also arresting you, Mrs Jones, for conspiracy to murder. That'll do to be going on with.' And as she spluttered denials and Frear led her from the room, he bent to pick up Malcolm's ring.

'So that's how it was,' Webb finished flatly, glancing at Una Bennett's impassive face. 'Rita Jones had built up a virulent hatred against Malcolm, blaming him for Lennie's death because she had to blame someone. The boy is weak, completely dominated by her, and seemed quite happy to fall in with her plans. He was also, of course, involved in the shop raids. I grant you they're an unlikely pair of villains, but none the less lethal for that.

'In fact, it was the boy, Dean, who heard you wanted a cleaner. It must have seemed like fate; Rita'd been wondering how to get her own back, now she was handed the opportunity. She says she considered using another name when she went to you, but decided it might get too complicated. In any case, "Jones" afforded her sufficient anonymity, and she was banking on the fact that Malcolm had never met her.

'Anyway, you took her on, she had a duplicate key made for the back door, and settled down to bide her time. Then fate gave her another nudge. Because she was early that Friday, she heard you both talking in the kitchen, and realized he'd be alone in the house the next day. It was almost too easy. Dean went along, let himself in and lay in wait. You were right – there was someone in the house when you came back for your blouse.'

She gave a small shiver but made no comment. After a glance at her face, Webb moved from the facts leading to her husband's murder to those surrounding Neil's.

'When Jones saw him pick up the ring,' he finished, 'he grabbed the knife from one of the other raiders – who, incidentally, fled up north when he realized what it had been used for; the Blackpool police are holding him. Jones swears it was only for intimidation, but I doubt if Neil even saw it; if he had, he wouldn't have turned his back.'

There was a short silence. Realizing he'd come to the end, Una looked up.

'Thank you, Mr Webb. I'm grateful to you for explaining everything.'

'Has the family been round?'

She shook her head.

'Would you like me – ?'

'No!'

'But you shouldn't be here alone, it can't – '

'I shan't be, much longer; there are a couple of properties I'm interested in, and I shall be moving shortly. As soon as probate comes through, this house will go on the market.'

'I see. Well, if there's anything I can do – '

She rose with him. 'Thank you, but I can manage. I always have done.'

She stood at the window, watching as he got into the car and drove away. It was Saturday morning. This time last week, she had been at the hairdresser's, realizing that she'd forgotten to collect her blouse from the airing-cupboard. Seven long days ago.

If she hadn't gone to the concert, if she hadn't engaged the poisonous Mrs Jones, would anything have been different? Or would they still have got Malcolm in the end?

Only one thing was certain; she couldn't allow that nebulous guilt to destroy her. She mourned Malcolm – part of her always would – but to be rational about it, she hadn't been particularly happy in her marriage. She'd felt constrained by his constant presence, by the hostility of the rest of the family, by having to remember to tell him if she'd be late home, and consequent reproachful silences.

Perhaps she'd lived alone too long to be able to adapt; the truth was that she was happiest being her own mistress, able to please herself without having to consider other people. Soon, she would move out of this house with its painful memories, and revert to using her maiden name. She would make a new start in the flat, or perhaps a 'restart', since everything would be as it was before.

One is one and all alone, and evermore shall be so.

Very well, she, 'Una-ique', would accept that role in life. She would, she felt confident, not only survive, but prosper.

Lifting her head and straightening her shoulders, she turned from the window. There was much to do.